PRAISE FOR ROBIN LEE HATCHER

"*Bible and a .44* is a story full of redemption and hope. Hope not only for wayward sons and daughters, but for the people who love them as well. With her gift of storytelling, Robin Lee Hatcher brings a Great Depression-era small town in Idaho to life, where a cast of characters live out a story that is both believable and inspiring, reminding us that no one is so lost they can't come home." — Michelle Shocklee, award-winning author of *All We Thought We Knew* and *Appalachian Song*

"In *Bible and a .44*, Robin Lee Hatcher crafts a moving story of uncertain homecomings, redemption, and the power of grace. With heartfelt storytelling and richly drawn characters, this novella beautifully captures the struggle of facing one's past and the freedom that comes with forgiveness. A tender and uplifting read, it's a reminder that no one is beyond the reach of love, faith, and second chances." ~ Karen Barnett, award-winning author of *Where Trees Touch the Sky* and the National Park Novels

"[*I Hope You Dance*] is classic sweet romance. Robin Lee Hatcher excels at creating memorable characters with true-to-life struggles and she delivers that here even with the shorter word count. And, oh my, the toe-curls!!!! And yay for a solid faith thread even with the novella length." — 5 star Goodreads review

"In [*I Hope You Dance*] we get to head to the country where life is a little more laid back. The barrel racing dance teacher is sure she will never find love. The country boy chef is sure he doesn't want love. We know the rest, the story that gets them there is so sweet." — 5 star Goodreads review

"Hatcher's newest novella offers the same sweet romance and page-turning storyline you've come to expect from this author if you've read her before. If you haven't, you're in for a treat! *To Enchant a Lady's Heart* is, in a word, well...*enchanting.*" — Deborah Raney, author of *Breath of Heaven* and *A Nest of Sparrows*

"The consequences of a long-ago romantic tryst come to light in this enjoyable historical [*I'll Be Seeing You*] by Hatcher. Brianna Hastings, an entitled college student, dreads interviewing her 98-year-old great-grandmother Daisy for a history project, but becomes gradually involved as Daisy reflects on her tumultuous love life during WWII ... Hatcher skillfully illustrates her message that God transforms bad into good for those with faith. WWII-era inspirational fans will relish this tale." — *Publishers Weekly*

FROM THIS MOMENT ON

FROM THIS MOMENT ON

TWO KINGS MEADOW NOVELLAS

ROBIN LEE HATCHER

A NOTE FROM THE AUTHOR

When I first created the town of Kings Meadow in my novel, *A Promise Kept*, I had no idea that it would become beloved by readers and become one of my favorite settings for stories. Three more novels and one novella set in Kings Meadow soon followed.

The novella that was set in Kings Meadow, *I Hope You Dance* (published in 2015), is still available as a stand-alone novella as well as being in the Year of Weddings collection called *Kiss the Bride*.

Ten years later, I found myself wishing I could set another story in Kings Meadow. And how perfect if it could be related in some way to the characters in *I Hope You Dance*. But when should it be set? In my existing novels, Kings Meadow's history went back to the gold rush days. Did I want to write something in the past or in the present? At first I couldn't decide. Then my hair stylist mentioned a country song to me, one that I hadn't heard before. The title was "Bible and a .44." It wasn't long before a story began to take shape in my imagination along with when it should take place.

I enjoyed my return to Kings Meadow in *Bible and a .44*, and I hope readers will love these two stories about the Foster family. Be sure to check out the simple family tree in the back of the book.

I love to hear from readers, so please stay in touch.

Robin

BIBLE AND A .44

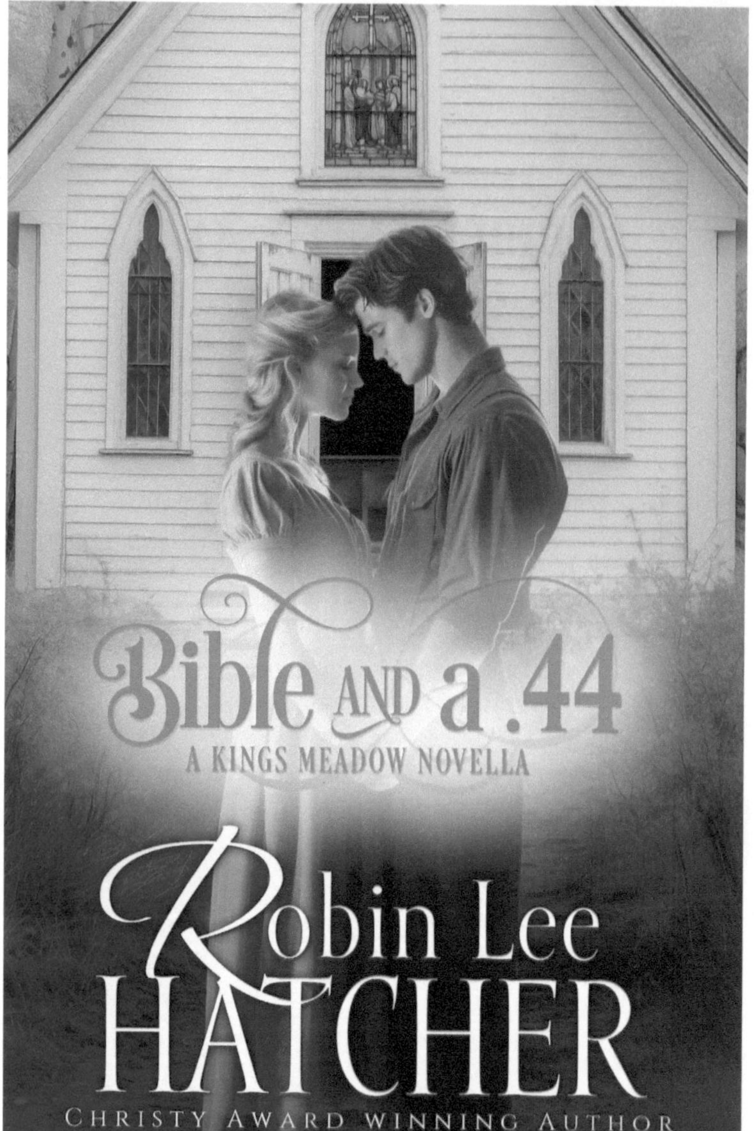

Bible AND a .44
A KINGS MEADOW NOVELLA
Robin Lee
HATCHER
CHRISTY AWARD WINNING AUTHOR

To Shannon. Thanks for the inspiration and the friendship!

1

Kings Meadow, Idaho
June 1932

Jesse Graham hopped off the truck bed and shouted, "Thanks," before the driver continued on his way, the old pickup backfiring twice as it rounded a bend in the road. Carrying his duffle bag—it held everything he owned, other than the clothes he wore—he began the mile-long walk into Kings Meadow.

Seven years had passed since he left the small town in the mountains north of Boise, helped on his way by the anger of Pastor Kinsey Foster. Nerves formed a knot in Jesse's belly at the notion of seeing the preacher—and his .44— again, and he stopped walking to take a few deep breaths. Then he gave himself a moment to admire the pine-covered mountains that rose on all sides of the wide valley. Heaven knew he'd missed this view. He'd seen some great country in his travels, but there was something about his hometown he

5

never forgot. He'd never stopped feeling the pull to return. And now, here he was.

Not that anyone besides his ma would be glad to see him, and even she might have reservations. He couldn't blame her. He'd been a hell-raiser from a young age, had gotten into more than his fair share of trouble, and had done nothing to make Ma's life easier. Raising a boy alone was hard for any woman. He'd made it even harder.

He wondered how she was doing. It shamed him that he didn't know the answer. But she didn't have a telephone, and he'd never stayed in one place long enough to have an address for her to use. Excuses. Those were merely excuses. A dutiful son would have returned to look after her. He hadn't been a dutiful son in the past. Not ever.

He was determined to be one now.

Of course, it wasn't only his ma he wanted to forgive him. He owed amends to more than a few folks, starting with the preacher man who carried a Bible along with his .44 revolver —and knew how to use both.

Jesse blew out a breath, then resumed the walk into town. The air was still, the temperature pleasant. Only birdsong broke the quiet of late afternoon. He heard no truck or car engines in the distance, no squeak and bang of farm machinery, no horses whinnying or stomping a hoof. It occurred to him suddenly that all might not be the same in Kings Meadow as when he left. It hadn't been a full three years since the stock market crashed and the entire country sank into an "economic situation," as President Hoover called it. A situation from which there seemed no way out. Jesse had become one of tens of thousands of men moving from place to place, trying to find work of any kind so they could feed themselves and feed their families.

Some might think the difficulty in finding employment had brought him home again, but it wasn't that. It was the living God who'd put an end to Jesse's wandering ways. One day he'd been a man set on doing things his own way and for his own pleasure, and the next he'd become a new creation, a bond-slave of Jesus Christ, called to walk according to His will and His ways.

The news would surprise those who'd known him in the past. But no one could be more surprised than Jesse Graham himself.

WILLOW FOSTER LOVED THE WAY THE JUNE LIGHT FELL ACROSS the valley and her grandparents' farm as afternoon worked its way toward evening. This hour of the day never failed to beckon her outside to breathe in the beauty of God's earth. Birds fluttered in the trees, singing joyfully, and bees buzzed around the flowers planted near the front porch of the house. Her grandpa's two work horses stood in the pasture, their heads hung low, their tails swishing at flies.

The serious heat of summer hadn't come to Kings Meadow yet, and glad of it, Willow turned her face to the sun, eyes closed. Softly, she sang, "For the beauty of the earth, / for the glory of the skies, / for the love which from our birth / over and around us lies."

Oakley, her Scottish terrier, nudged her behind one knee to get her attention.

"Lord of all, to thee we raise / this our hymn of grateful praise."

The dog's nose butted her again, harder this time.

She laughed as she opened her eyes. "Okay. Okay. I know." She leaned down to stroke the dog's head. "I'd best be getting back inside. Grandpa will be home soon and supper isn't ready."

She spun around and walked toward the sun-bleached house that had been her home for nearly fourteen years, ever since the death of her parents from the Spanish Flu. That was when Willow, nine at the time, had come with her twelve-year-old brother, Craig, to live with Grandpa and Grandma Foster. Now, all these years later, Craig was serving as a medical corpsman in the US Army, stationed at Fort Sam Houston in Texas, while Willow had never ventured farther from Kings Meadow than Idaho's capital city. And oddly enough, she was content. She'd never yearned to see the world, only to be at home in her small corner of it.

As she opened the side door, she called out, "Grandma?"

"I'm here, dear," came the weak reply.

Willow passed through the kitchen and stepped into the front parlor. Her grandma sat in the rocking chair, a quilt covering her from ankles to throat, gnarled fingers folded over her stomach as she looked out the window with watery blue eyes.

"Is your grandpa home?"

"Not yet." She kissed Grandma on the forehead. "But he should be soon. The meatloaf's about ready to come out of the oven. I've still got the potatoes to mash." She gave the older woman another quick peck, this time on the cheek, before returning to the kitchen.

After washing her hands, she set to work, finishing the last of the meal preparation. Everything was ready to go onto the table when the kitchen door opened and her grandpa stepped into the house.

Kinsey Foster was a tall man, thinner now at seventy-one than he'd been a decade before, but there was steel in his spine. Gray streaks had lightened his once dark hair. Willow thought him handsome, even at his age, and a kinder man she'd never met. He preached the gospel with fire and zeal while shepherding his flock with compassion and joy.

"You're right on time," she said.

"Smells mighty good in here."

She smiled. Grandpa said that every evening when he came home. "It's meatloaf." Of course, she had stretched the meat with plenty of breadcrumbs, but the generous use of ketchup would help hide that fact.

"And how's your grandma today?"

"About the same. But feeling up to sitting in the rocker. You'll find her in the parlor."

He nodded, his expression grim. "I'd best say hello to her."

Willow's throat tightened with emotion. Her grandparents' love for and devotion to each other had been such an example of how marriage should be. Grandma had always shown her husband respect and honor, and Grandpa was the type of man who would lay down his life for his wife, loving her the way Christ loved the church. But Grandma wasn't well. Life seemed to drain from her body a little more each day. She ate like a bird, and nothing Willow cooked tempted her to eat more.

"When she stops eating and drinking altogether, it won't

be long," Dr. Bunch had said the last time he came to see Grandma.

Willow glanced into the parlor. Grandpa sat on a stool next to the rocking chair. He held one of Grandma's hands and stroked the back of it with his thumb as he bowed his head and said a prayer.

"Amen," Willow whispered when Grandpa looked up again, his gaze adoring the face of his wife.

A short while later, the three of them sat at the kitchen table. Even though her grandma ate little, she joined them at the table when she was able. Willow was grateful Grandma could sit with them today.

After Grandpa thanked God for the food He'd provided, Willow spooned some mashed potatoes onto the plate in front of her grandma while Grandpa helped himself to the meatloaf. After they had passed the serving dishes around, Grandpa and Willow started eating. Grandma just stared at the food on her plate without interest.

Eventually, Grandpa broke the silence. "Heard a bit of interesting news on my way home."

Willow looked up expectantly.

"Jesse Graham's back in Kings Meadow."

The food in her stomach turned to stone.

"Max Johnson saw him walking down Main Street earlier. Looked like he was on his way to Maud's house."

"Was Mr. Johnson sure it was him?"

"He was sure." Grandpa laid down his fork and gave her a long look. "Does it trouble you that he's returned?"

She lifted her chin. "It doesn't trouble me if he's back. I haven't given Jesse a second thought in years."

"Hmm." Her grandpa took up his fork and resumed eating.

He had a right to be skeptical. At sixteen, Willow had been head-over-heels in love with Kings Meadow's well-known rebel, and she'd been devastated when he left town. But she wasn't that same naive girl with her head in a romantic cloud. Seven years had seen to that. She was over the hurt he'd left in his wake. She'd grown up and her feet were firmly planted on the ground. It didn't matter to her if he was back in town. Not one bit.

2

Jesse's boyhood bedroom looked exactly the same as the day he'd left it. Ma hadn't moved a thing in the years he'd been away. The same clothes hung in the small closet and filled the bureau drawers. The same pair of boots was tucked underneath the foot of the bed. The same comb and brush lay next to the same pitcher and washbasin on the same stand in the corner.

But Jesse wasn't the same, and he needed his ma and others in this town to know that.

The next morning, after washing, shaving, and dressing, he left his room and went into the kitchen where he stoked the fire in the cook stove, then prepared a pot of coffee before frying strips of bacon and scrambling a few eggs. It was gratifying to see the look on Ma's face when she joined him as he moved the eggs to the waiting plates on the counter.

"You cooked breakfast, son?"

"I did." He grinned. "Turns out, I'm not a bad cook, if I have the right provisions."

"Those can be hard to come by these days."

That sobered his thoughts. "How are you getting on, Ma? Do you have enough money? Have you had to do without? You didn't say last night."

In truth, she hadn't said much of anything last night. As soon as she'd seen him, she'd embraced him and burst into tears. And she'd started to cry again every time he asked a question. Finally, he'd been content to sit with her in silence, his arm around her shoulders.

"I didn't say because I was so happy to see you," she answered now.

Jesse carried the plates of bacon and eggs to the table, then he poured coffee into a couple of cups and delivered those too.

"It's good to be back home." They sat at the table, Jesse taking the chair opposite her. "And I'm here to stay, the good Lord willing. But now tell me. How are you getting on? Really."

"I do all right. I've got my sewing work to bring in a little income, and I get fresh vegetables and milk from our neighbors. There's never been a lack of generosity in the people of Kings Meadow. Not even in these hard times. And the chickens are faithful to lay their eggs, just like they're supposed to. Truth is, I don't always have what I want, but God sees that I've got what I need."

"He's done the same for me. Even when I'm faithless, He's faithful."

Questions filled her eyes as she looked at him.

"Is it okay if I say the blessing over the meal?"

The questions left her eyes, replaced by a glitter of tears.

He bowed his head and thanked God for keeping both of them safe in their years apart, then thanked Him for the food set before them, and ended with, "Please guide our steps today and always, Lord. In the name of Your Son, Jesus, I pray. Amen."

"Amen," Ma whispered.

He gave her a smile, then took up his fork and made quick work of the eggs and bacon on his plate, washing the food down with the strong, black coffee.

There'd been plenty of mornings, especially in the last couple of years, when he would have considered this a meal fit for a king. He'd gone to sleep hungry more than once, and he'd woken up even hungrier. He'd stood in more than one soup line, and he'd stuffed old newspapers in the bottoms of his shoes. He hoped what his ma said was true. He hoped she'd never had to go hungry like he had or do without anything important.

"Tell me your story, son."

He met her gaze. "My story?"

"It's clear something's changed in you. Something more than you getting seven years older and seeing a bit of the country. What really brought you back to Kings Meadow?"

"You're right. I've got a story to tell. It took some hard knocks and some near misses, but Jesus finally got my attention out there on the road."

The tears swam in her eyes once more. "Hallelujah."

"And amen."

She reached across the table and took hold of his hand, silently giving his fingers a squeeze.

"I've come back to Kings Meadow to set things right. I've

got more people than just you who I need to ask forgiveness from. But I'm starting with you. I'm sorry for what I did, and I'm asking for your forgiveness."

"You've got it already. You don't even need to ask."

"Maybe not. But I want to ask, all the same. You know I'll need to prove myself to people hereabouts. To anyone who knew me, I reckon. But I'm willing to do what I need to let them see I'm a different man today."

"You were a boy when you left."

"I wasn't a boy. Young, maybe, but not a boy. And I was angry and thoughtless and selfish." He took a breath. "And full of rotgut too much of the time."

Ma could do little but nod in agreement.

He pushed back his chair from the table. "I'm going to see Pastor Foster this morning. Then I'll look for a job anywhere in town. Or maybe on one of the farms or at the Leonard Ranch." He knew jobs were hard to come by. His ma knew the same, but neither of them admitted it out loud. As he stood, he added, "I'll wash the dishes before I go."

"Never you mind the dishes. I'll do them. I do some of my best praying with my hands in soapy water."

Jesse leaned over and kissed the top of her head. "Love you, Ma."

"Love you, too, son."

THE HINGES ON THE FRONT DOOR TO THE CHURCH CREAKED AS Kinsey Foster entered the building. Every morning he heard that sound and told himself to bring the oil can with him the next time. But by tomorrow he would likely forget, just as he had every other day. Maybe his forgetfulness was because of age or maybe it was because oiling hinges wasn't his highest priority. Either way, the hinge continued to creak.

He moved through the small narthex and into the sanctuary. Soft morning light fell through the east-facing windows. Dust motes floated lazily in the air, an oddly comforting sight. He walked down the center aisle and took his usual seat in the front left pew. Once settled, he opened his Bible on his lap. He didn't turn to any particular page, and he didn't start to read. First, he closed his eyes and sought the Lord's presence.

"Excuse me," came a man's voice from the back of the sanctuary. "I'd like to speak to you, Pastor Foster, if you've got the time."

Kinsey didn't recognize the voice, although that didn't matter. He would give whoever it was what time he had. That had always been his way. He moved the Bible off his lap, rose, and turned.

Surprise shot through him. He'd heard Jesse Graham was back in town. Had even mentioned it to his wife and granddaughter. But it was still a shock to see him. The years had matured his face and broadened his shoulders. They'd added a few inches to his height as well. His thick, black hair was in need of a trim. His clothes were worn but clean. But what caught Kinsey's notice was something in the younger man's dark eyes. Even from the opposite end of the sanctuary, he sensed the changes in Jesse were far more than physical.

"Jesse Graham." He spoke the name softly.

"Hello, pastor."

"Never thought we'd see you in Kings Meadow again."

"I never thought you would either. Especially after the way we parted."

Hat held between his hands, Jesse moved slowly down the center aisle, almost as if afraid he wasn't welcome in church. His uncertainty was warranted, given the last time they'd seen each other. That night, in Kinsey's rage, he'd wanted to break more than one of the Ten Commandments, including committing murder. In truth, he had threatened to do just that.

Kinsey cleared his throat. "You found your mother well, I trust."

"Yes, sir. I did. Thank the good Lord. And thank you. I reckon you've done more than your share to help her."

Kinsey motioned toward the pew across the aisle.

Jesse sat as directed. He looked over at Kinsey for a short while, then raised his eyes to the cross on the wall behind the pulpit. Kinsey sank onto his own pew and waited. He was good at waiting.

"After Pa died," Jesse began softly, "I was an angry kid. Not that I understood it at the time. But I was. Angry with Pa for dying, even though it wasn't his fault he got sick. I was angry with him for leaving us to make it on our own. I was angry at the God you preached about and the one Ma trusted. Ma did her best to keep me in line. You know she did. Everybody in town knew it, I reckon. After I got my first taste of moonshine, she didn't have a hope of controlling me. She was no match for my stubborn will."

None of that was news to Kinsey. He'd had a front row seat to watch it happen.

"Pastor, I need to say I'm sorry and to ask for your forgiveness."

Kinsey nodded but didn't look in Jesse's direction. Just waited for the young man to keep speaking his piece.

"You could have done more to me than wave your .44 and tell me to get out of town. No one would've blamed you if you had." Jesse drew in a deep breath and released it. "Speaking of that night, I owe an apology to Willow, too, and if she'll let me say it to her face, I'd like to."

Kinsey's jaw clenched. Was that a good idea? His granddaughter had said it didn't matter to her that Jesse had returned. But was that true? He remembered her devastation as if it happened yesterday. She'd grown up a lot, but he sensed a wounded corner of her heart that had never been exposed to the light.

"I wish I could tell you I wised up right after I left here, pastor, but I didn't. I just kept going downward, getting into more trouble, spending time in places and with people who weren't good for me. I should have died more than once. Guess it's a miracle I didn't."

Silence fell over the sanctuary, a silence that lasted so long it forced Kinsey to look across the aisle again. He found the younger man staring right back at him.

"I lived that way right up until I met a man in a shantytown in California. Right about a year ago now. I can't tell you what it was about Paul Simpson that made me listen when I hadn't listened to anybody else, including you. Pastor Foster, I saw Jesus in him. I don't know how else to say it. And once I saw Jesus, I began to see the devil in myself."

Kinsey rarely cried, but tears blinded him now. Mostly from shame because Jesse hadn't seen Jesus in him long before. Jesse had to go far from home to see it in a stranger.

"Paul and me, we would sit by the campfire at night, and

he'd tell me different stories from the Bible and about what God had revealed to him through the words he read in it. One day, I knew I wanted to live for God instead of for myself. I confessed my sins right then, and Paul baptized me in the ocean. I don't know how to describe what happened except to say I came up out of those waters a new creature in Christ. Just like the Bible says."

The lump in Kinsey's throat kept him from speaking, so he settled for a nod.

"I'm back home to make amends for the wrongs I committed. And to be the right kind of son for Ma. To honor her like I'm supposed to." He rose from the pew. "Guess that's all I came to say." He set the battered brown hat on his head and started down the aisle.

"Jesse." Kinsey stood and turned. "I'm willing to forgive you. But I . . . Just be careful with my granddaughter."

"I will be, sir. I give you my word."

Kinsey could only pray the young man's word had become worth something.

3

The morning sunlight reflected off a white sheet on the clothesline, nearly blinding Willow as she hung the last of the wash. When the task was finished, she picked up the empty basket near her feet and turned toward the house. But she stopped at the sight of the man in the center of the path between her and the door. Maybe her heart stopped beating too. At least it felt that way.

"Hello, Willow."

She gripped the wicker basket a little tighter against her side. "Jesse. I heard you were back."

Oakley ran forward to sniff the new arrival, his tail wagging furiously. Did the dog recognize Jesse after such a long time?

Jesse bent over and patted the dog's head. "Hello, Oakley." He straightened again, his gaze on Willow.

"Are you staying long?" she asked, voice tight.

"Plan to."

"Your ma must be glad."

"She is." He swept the hat off his head and raked the fingers of one hand through his hair, pushing it back from his face.

Mercy, he was even more handsome now than he'd been before. His skin was bronzed by the sun. He looked taller, leaner, stronger than before. His dark hair was longer now, shaggy, and it somehow suited him. Her heart palpitated, the same way it used to whenever she was with him. Her mouth went dry, and her lips tingled. Years ago she'd welcomed those feelings, but not now.

"I went to see your grandpa at the church."

Irritation replaced unwelcome attraction. "Didn't you fear lightning would strike you dead, going into a church?"

One corner of his mouth curved slightly. "No."

Lightning should have struck him. It should have struck him dead. He deserved nothing less.

"Willow, I'm sorry for the hurt I caused you."

"You didn't cause any hurt." It was a lie, but she didn't care. Her pride wouldn't let her speak the truth.

"I'm sorry, Willow. Truly sorry. And I'd like to ask your forgiveness."

"Forgiveness?" She'd told Grandpa she hadn't given Jesse a second thought, but that was a lie too. She *had* thought about him. Often. He'd hurt her, but she wouldn't be fool enough to let him hurt her again.

"I don't expect you to forgive me now," he said, his voice low. "But I hope some day you will."

She lifted her chin high, refusing to say another word. Angry at herself for noticing his good looks. Angry at her heart for reacting at the sight of him. Angry because she hadn't sent him packing the instant he entered the yard.

He set the hat over his hair again, gave her a nod, and turned away. She watched him follow the path back to the road, a strange sadness washing over her.

Why? Why the sadness? Why the anger? Jesse meant nothing to her. The past was the past. She was over him. She might have thought about him through the years. She might recognize the hurt he'd caused. But those were just memories. She was better now. She was happier.

She huffed out a breath as she returned to the house, Oakley at her heels once again. After setting the basket on the floor in the washroom, she went to the kitchen sink, filled the kettle with water, and set it on the stove to boil. Then she went to her grandparents' bedroom, rapping softly on the half-open door before entering.

"Grandma? I'm going to fix a cup of tea. Would you like one?"

The older woman opened her eyes. "No, dear. I don't need a thing."

"Would you like to get up and sit in your rocker?"

"No." The word sounded more like a sigh. "I think I'll stay in bed for now."

Her grandma appeared much weaker today than yesterday, and Willow's heart squeezed in response. "I'm done with the wash." She took another step into the bedroom. "Would you like me to read to you for a while?"

Grandma's eyes drifted closed again. "That would be nice, dear."

"I'll get my tea and be right back."

When she returned to the bedroom, cup of tea in hand, she thought her grandma was sound asleep. But her eyes fluttered open before Willow reached the chair beside the bed. After taking a sip of tea, she placed the cup next to several books on a small, nearby table. "What story do you want to hear?"

"*The Adventures of Tom Sawyer*," Grandma answered without hesitation.

Willow pulled the book from the stack and opened it. She'd read it so often that she'd nearly memorized the beginning of the story. Still, she looked down at the page as she began to read aloud:

"Tom!" No answer. "TOM!" No answer. "What's gone with that boy, I wonder? You TOM!" No answer. The old lady pulled her spectacles down and looked over them about the room; then she put them up and looked out under them. She seldom or never looked through them for so small a thing as a boy; they were her state pair, the pride of her heart, and were built for "style," not service—she could have seen through a pair of stove-lids just as well.

Grandma chuckled. "Seeing through a pair of stove-lids. I never."

"I agree." Willow touched her grandma's shoulder.

"Always was glad the Lord let me keep seeing without needing glasses. Kinsey is always and forever losing his."

"I know."

"He needs you to help keep track of them. The way I used to for him."

Her throat constricted. "I know."

"Keep reading, dear. I'll just close my eyes and listen. You have the prettiest reading voice."

Willow swallowed the lump in her throat and turned her eyes to the book on her lap and began to read again:

She looked perplexed for a moment, and then said, not fiercely, but still loud enough for the furniture to hear: "Well, I lay if I get hold of you I'll..."

It was her grandma's soft snores—two chapters later—that caused Willow to close the book and set it next to the cold cup of tea on the table.

"Love you." She leaned forward and kissed her grandma's forehead, then rose and left the bedroom.

The respite found while reading to her grandma had quieted her—heart and soul—but as she began to sweep the parlor floor, memories of Jesse Graham crept into her thoughts, disturbing the temporary peace she'd found.

***

JESSE HADN'T PAID MUCH ATTENTION TO THE BUILDINGS ON Main Street when he'd walked through town the previous day, but he paid attention now. Prohibition had closed the old tavern more than a decade before. The building still stood empty and unused after all this time. But despite the crisis oppressing the nation, most of the other businesses in Kings Meadow seemed to be holding on.

There was the general store that also housed the post office. Sandwiched between the general store and the Twilight Cafe was the butcher shop. The barbershop was open, Todd Hanson's name still above the door. If Jesse could have afforded it, he'd have gone in for a haircut. But he couldn't afford it. On down the street, he saw someone loading the back of a wagon outside the Kings Meadow Feed Store, and opposite it was Sal Kent's livery and blacksmith shop, although it seemed to have partially transitioned to a garage for automobile and other engine repairs. He wondered if the sawmill was still in operation. Located about half a mile north of the town, the mill might be the place he was most apt to find employment.

Jesse had become a jack of all trades during his years away. He could wrestle cattle and shear sheep. He could sell soap from behind a counter. He knew how to pick apples and harvest grapes and bale hay. Of course, folks in Kings Meadow might not believe he'd done any of those things. The last they'd seen of him, he hadn't been good for much except causing trouble.

He turned his gaze toward the general store. He might as well begin there.

A bell over the door chimed as he entered, and several heads turned in his direction.

Susan Johnson stood behind the counter with her husband, Max. They looked the same as the last time he'd seen them, right down to the sour expression on Susan's face.

"Well, I'll be," Max said. "Jesse Graham. I thought that was you I saw yesterday, but the missus here told me it couldn't be. No way would you ever be back."

Jesse reckoned he would hear similar words again and again in the coming days. "It's me." He bumped the brim of his hat, pushing it off his forehead. "I'm back to stay, and I'm hoping to find work to help out Ma."

"You want to work in our store?" Susan turned toward her husband, as if wanting him to say the request was ridiculous. They wouldn't want the likes of him anywhere near their merchandise or their till.

Jesse answered, "If you've got a job for me, I'm interested."

"We don't." She crossed her arms over her chest.

Max's expression held a touch of sympathy. "Sorry, Jesse. We've got no need of an extra hand. You know how things are."

"Yeah, I know how they are." He tugged his hat forward again. "Thanks anyway. I appreciate the consideration."

Outside on the boardwalk, Jesse paused, facing west. Earlier that morning, Pastor Foster—who had more reasons than anyone to dislike him—had freely given his forgiveness. Jesse had known it wouldn't be that easy with others. After all, a pastor's job was to demonstrate the way one was supposed to live. But people might sit in church and still not take those lessons to heart.

He took a deep breath and let it out as he moved on. He didn't bother to inquire in the butcher shop. Arnold Hirsch had always run a one-man business, and Jesse didn't imagine that had changed. He bypassed the cafe as well. He could cook, but he doubted they would want him in place of a waitress. If he failed everywhere else, then he might return to the cafe. The barber shop was another pass. He didn't think anybody in Kings Meadow would want him taking scissors to their hair, especially when he could use a haircut himself.

He stopped walking outside the Kings Meadow Press. Newton Smith, the owner and editor of the weekly newspaper used to have a soft spot for Jesse's widowed ma, and that soft spot had spilled over onto Jesse as a boy. Maybe Newton would take that into consideration.

He opened the door and was met immediately by the sharp, metallic tang of printer's ink mixed with the dusty, woody aroma of paper. Added to it was the scent of tobacco.

Newton Smith had rarely ever been seen without his pipe. Jesse assumed that remained true.

"Have a seat," a voice called from the back room. "Be right with you."

Jesse removed his hat but didn't sit. Instead, he let his gaze roam over the large front room of the newspaper office. To the right was a sturdy wooden desk, scuffed and worn from years of use. On one side of the desk was a typewriter, a sheet of paper rising above its roller. Filing cabinets lined the wall, newspapers stacked on top of them. Shelves held books, spare typewriter ribbons, and reams of paper. To the right stood the bulky, cast-iron printing press. It was surrounded by trays of metal type. Ink rollers and stacks of freshly printed newspapers were scattered about. Hanging on the wall was a large calendar.

"What can I do for—" Newton stopped abruptly. The smile he'd worn faded. "Jesse Graham."

He sounded a lot like Pastor Foster. Not so much surprised as resigned. Seemed like the soft spot hadn't stuck around.

"Hello, Mr. Smith."

"I heard you were back."

"Yes, sir. I'm back to look after Ma."

The man stuck his pipe in the corner of his mouth. "Do tell."

"In order to do that, I'm going to need some kind of employment."

"Would seem so." Newton struck a match and held it to the bowl of the pipe while he puffed on the mouthpiece.

"Have you got any work I might do? I'm willing to do anything. Anything at all."

Silence filled the office. A long, uncomfortable silence. Jesse expected to be turned away. It was nothing less than he deserved, and most folks had long memories.

"Yes," Newton said with a nod. "I think I could use you."

Jesse blinked in disbelief. "Really?"

Newton grunted as he moved to his desk chair and sat on it, still puffing on his pipe. "You ever worked for a newspaper?"

"No, sir."

"What have you done the last seven years?"

"A little of everything. Well, not everything. But lots of different things. I'm a quick learner."

"That's good because you'll be doing a little of everything that needs done around here. Starting with sweeping the floor. Think you can manage that?"

He still couldn't quite believe it. "Yes, sir." Maybe that soft spot hadn't disappeared entirely.

Newton pointed to the rear of the office. "You'll find the broom, dustpan, and an apron in the back room." He hesitated a moment, then added, "Go on. Get to it. Time's a wasting."

With a silent prayer of thanks—he recognized a miracle when one happened to him—Jesse followed Newton's orders.

4

Willow was setting a straw hat onto her head when she heard Ethel Brubaker's knock on the kitchen door. She didn't bother to call down to the woman. Ethel always let herself in after knocking. The woman would stop long enough to pour herself a cup of coffee and then go to check on Grandma. It was the same every Sunday.

Most people within riding or walking distance of Willow Creek Chapel attended church on a Sunday morning, but Ethel Brubaker wasn't one of them. She didn't hold with religion, as she was quick to tell anyone who asked, as well as a few of those who didn't. However, she'd been Grandma's dear friend for over forty years, and now that Grandma wasn't able to attend church services with her preacher husband and their granddaughter, Ethel had made it her responsibility to come spend as much of the day with her as necessary.

Willow took up her Bible from the table beside the bed

and left the room. "Good morning, Mrs. Brubaker," she called softly as she descended the narrow staircase.

"Morning, Willow. Your grandpa already over at the church?" She asked the same thing every Sunday.

And every Sunday, Willow answered, "Yes. He goes early."

"That man doesn't know how to rest. Doesn't your good book say something about getting rest?"

"Yes, ma'am. It does. But Grandpa finds his rest in Jesus."

Ethel harrumphed. "He would say that. Well, you go on with your Sunday duties. I'm here now."

"Thank you, Mrs. Brubaker. Grandpa and I appreciate your kindness."

"Roberta would do the same for me if she was able."

Willow answered with a smile. Ethel couldn't have said anything more true about her grandma. Roberta Foster had always been quick to do a good deed for a friend or a neighbor. Same for a stranger, truth be told.

The walk from the Foster farm to the church wasn't a long one, but it was one Willow enjoyed in good weather. Moments of peace when she could gather her thoughts and pray for those she loved, especially her grandparents. It was hard enough knowing that Grandma wouldn't long be with them. It was even harder knowing what the loss would mean to Grandpa.

"Comfort him now, Lord," she whispered. "And comfort him then."

She rounded a bend in the road, and the church came into sight. Other congregants walked toward it too, which meant she was late. Grandpa depended upon her to help welcome his flock on Sunday mornings. She quickened her footsteps but stopped a few strides later when she saw who was talking to her grandpa on the church steps.

Jesse Graham.

At church.

On a Sunday.

And God still hadn't struck him dead.

Grandpa noticed her first. Then Jesse turned his head to look in her direction. And when their gazes met, a memory washed over her, one she had determined never to think of again. She saw her younger self with Jesse in the shadow-filled barn, her lips burning from his kisses, her body aching for his touch, her heart believing he loved her too. If only—

She lowered her eyes and set her jaw. She wouldn't remember it. She wouldn't think about the past. She wouldn't. When she looked again, Jesse was no longer beside Grandpa. Had he left? Probably. He'd never been one for church. She forced a smile and crossed the remaining distance.

"Sorry I'm late, Grandpa."

He gave a nod. "Mrs. Brubaker get there all right?"

"Yes. Grandma's in good hands."

Grandpa was silent a short while, his gaze intent. Finally, he asked, "Are you all right?"

She knew at once that Jesse hadn't walked away from the church while her eyes were lowered. Instead, he'd gone inside. He was in there now. "I'm fine, Grandpa. Don't you worry about me."

Abe Leonard and his family approached the church entrance, and Willow was glad to turn, along with her grandpa, to greet them. Anything to keep her thoughts off Jesse.

MOST FOLKS HAD THEIR USUAL PLACE TO SIT IN CHURCH, including Jesse's ma. When he saw her in the last pew on the left, he knew she'd done that for him. She'd chosen to sit there so he wouldn't have people staring at the back of his head and wondering about him. He'd avoided church like the plague as a boy so there would be plenty of surprise to go around, folks noticing he'd turned up on his first Sunday back in Kings Meadow.

He sat next to his ma, resting his Bible on one thigh.

"It's good to have you in church with me," she said softly.

"It's good to be with you. I mean it, Ma. It's good."

But then he thought of the look on Willow's face when she'd seen him. She wouldn't agree that his presence was a good thing, and he couldn't blame her. Not really. Pastor Foster had told him to be careful with her, and he'd promised he would be. But what did that mean? He wanted to make amends to everyone he'd harmed, and Willow was at the top of that list. But how was he to make amends when she could barely look at him?

Regret pricked his heart. It didn't seem to matter that there was no condemnation to those who were in Christ Jesus, like the Bible told him. Maybe he wasn't condemned, but regret lingered all the same. Sometimes the shame from his past felt too much to bear.

"Son?"

He blinked before turning his head to look at Ma.

"We walk it out in faith. Each day. Each moment. And He never leaves us or forsakes us."

Emotion welling in his throat, he nodded.

Little by little, the pews in the sanctuary filled. Jesse recognized most everybody who walked down the aisle to take their seats. Parents of kids he'd gone to school with as well as the kids themselves, all of them grown up. Some had changed a lot. Others looked much the same.

Willow was among the last to find her place. Front pew, left side of aisle. The same place she used to sit next to her grandma and older brother, Craig. Jesse remembered that from those rare times his ma succeeded in getting him to church.

Pastor Foster stepped to the pulpit and motioned with his hands as he said, "Let's rise and sing, 'O For a Thousand Tongues.'"

Susan Johnson played a few opening chords on the pump organ, and then the congregation joined in. "'O for a thousand tongues to sing / my great Redeemer's praise, / the glories of my God and King, / the triumphs of His grace.'"

Jesse let the words of the hymn wash over him. God's grace. It was amazing. It was triumphant. He could depend upon it.

"He puts your sin away from you as far as the east is from the west." As Paul Simpson's words played once again in Jesse's memory, he felt the shame loosen its tentacles on his heart and soul. He closed his eyes and prayed that God would continue to reveal truth to him, to change him to be a little more like Jesus each and every day.

When the hymn was done, the congregation settled back onto the pews with a rustle of skirts and shuffle of feet.

"Welcome," Pastor Foster said with a smile. "Welcome to the house of God on this glorious Sunday morning. Would you bow your heads and join me in saying the Lord's Prayer."

KINSEY FOSTER NEVER STOOD STILL BEHIND A PULPIT. FROM his earliest days of preaching the word of God in the house of the Lord, he'd been a man on the move, striding from one side of the dais to the other. He didn't need to look at notes, although he always preached with his Bible open in one hand.

This morning's message was taken from the eighth chapter of Romans. For several weeks, he'd felt God impressing him to preach on the passage—from the first verse of the chapter to the last. He knew there was gold to be mined from the words the Apostle Paul wrote. Perhaps God meant the message for the young man in the back pew who'd returned to Kings Meadow, seeking forgiveness from those he'd harmed. Or perhaps it was for the young woman in the front pew, someone who needed to let go of the hurt she still carried, even though she did her best to hide and deny it. More than likely, the beloved chapter was for his entire congregation as well as for himself. God knew.

After the conclusion of the sermon, his flock rose to sing a final hymn, and he prayed that it was well with the souls of all his flock, that each person in the sanctuary would know the peace of Christ because they belonged to and trusted in Him.

With the final notes of the song lingering in the air, he spoke a benediction over them, and they began to depart.

He remained at the front of the sanctuary longer than usual, watching as various members of the congregation stopped to talk to Jesse and Maud Graham. Seeing their kindness pleased him.

"It's a surprise to see him in church," Newton Smith said, stepping to Kinsey's side.

"Yes. A good surprise."

"He's working for me at the paper."

Kinsey looked at the other man. "You hired Jesse?"

"Yep. A few days ago."

"I hadn't heard."

"It'll get around soon enough, I expect."

"What's he doing for you?"

"Just cleaning things up for now. Not sure what else he'll do. Depends how he gets on."

Kinsey rubbed his jaw. "He really means to stay in Kings Meadow. I wasn't sure when he told me, but I guess he does."

"Maud's glad to have him back. Look at her. Haven't seen her smile like that in years."

Kinsey did as Newton asked, and he had to agree. Maud Graham looked happy. Way deep down in her soul happy. And that happiness had taken a decade off her appearance. God bless her.

And God bless Jesse for being the cause of it.

5

———

Late on Monday afternoon, Jesse bid Newton a good night and began the walk toward home. Kings Meadow was quiet at this hour of the day, the warm air of early summer making the town feel sleepy and peaceful.

He had almost reached the general store when he heard men's voices—loud and coarse—coming from across the street near the old tavern. He didn't have to see the men to know that drinking of spirits was involved. He could hear it in their words. Prohibition had been the law of the land since early in 1920. While the law banned the manufacture, sale, and transportation of alcoholic beverages, it didn't criminalize the possession or consumption of it for personal use. And those who wanted to drink always found a way to purchase alcohol, most often the stuff made from an illegal still somewhere within walking or driving distance. And with the drinking came intoxication and trouble. Trouble he didn't want or need.

He kept walking and wouldn't have looked across the

street. But someone shouted his name, followed by a string of curse words. Now, he stopped and looked as Ben Travers stumbled out of the shadows between the tavern and the law office of Daniel Hoover. He was followed by two other men in the same inebriated condition, men Jesse didn't recognize.

"I heard you was back," Ben said, "but I didn't believe it."

"Hi, Ben." Jesse gave an abrupt nod of his head.

"Hi? Is that all you got to say to me after all this time? *Hi?*"

"What else is there to say?"

"You could say, 'I've got the money I took when I left town.' You must be here to pay me back. Can't think of any other reason."

"I didn't take anything with me that belonged to you."

Ben released another string of curses, staggering slightly to one side, as if knocked off balance by the force of his words. His hands balled into fists at his sides, evidence he was itching for a fight.

Recompense to no man evil for evil.

"Take care of yourself, Ben." Jesse turned on his heel and walked quickly away. He didn't want to find himself in an altercation in the middle of town. The old Jesse wouldn't have cared, but the new Jesse did. If Ben came after him in his current state, he didn't doubt he could handle him. But he didn't want to fight. He wanted to live in peace, if it was up to him. Better to be on his way and let Ben sober up before they met again.

But would he find Ben sober in the future? Maybe not. Ben had always liked his liquor. As a kid, Ben used to drink with his pa, and they hadn't hesitated to share their rotgut whiskey with Jesse, even though he was only about twelve at the time. Drinking strong spirits had been just one of the many bad choices Jesse had made back then.

He glanced over his shoulder, relieved to see no one followed. If he had it his way, he would avoid seeing Ben forever, although he knew that wouldn't happen in a town of this size.

Do I need to ask him to forgive me? The small voice in his spirit stopped him as certainly as when he'd heard Ben call his name. *Did* he need to ask his old drinking pal for forgiveness? That seemed preposterous. Ben had led the way into all kinds of trouble, mostly because he was three years older. He'd been the one to suggest breaking into the general store. He'd been the one to suggest taking old man Anderson's horse and turning it loose across the river. He'd been the one who—

Jesse frowned. Was that true? Had those been Ben's fault alone? No matter whose idea, Jesse had gone along willingly. Deflecting responsibility onto someone else wasn't the answer. Trying to live God's way was, but it wasn't easy. He'd learned that in the months since he found salvation. It was like the Apostle Paul wrote in one of his letters. Jesse wanted to do right but often ended up doing what he didn't want to do. He wanted his mind to be renewed but too often found himself thinking the old way, the wrong way.

He recalled the night Reverend Foster told him to get out of town. He'd seen the reality in the older man's eyes—as well as the .44 revolver stuck in the waistband of the pastor's trousers. Willow's grandpa was a man of peace, but he believed in justice too, and Jesse knew justice would fall hard if he didn't make himself scarce. So he'd thrown a few belongings into a knapsack, taken what cash was in the sock drawer in his ma's bedroom, and hightailed it out of Kings Meadow. No, he hadn't taken any money that belonged to Ben Travers, but he had stolen from Ma. The memory of that stung deep down in a secret place of his soul.

Drawing a breath, he resumed the walk toward home, then stopped again when he saw Willow Foster coming toward him, the handle of a basket hanging from the crook of one arm.

WILLOW FELT HER PULSE QUICKEN AND HER MOUTH GO DRY AT the sight of Jesse. She'd avoided him at church yesterday, before and after the service. She couldn't avoid him now.

"Evenin', Willow."

The timbre of his voice—deeper now than it had been years ago—seemed to reverberate inside her.

"Were you calling on Widow Blaine?"

"Yes." How had he known that? The Blaine house wasn't the only one down this road.

"I hope she's feeling better. I chopped wood for her on Saturday, and she was feeling a might poorly then."

"You chopped wood for her?"

He shrugged. "When I walked by her place the other day, I saw how low the wood pile was. Figured I could help her out that way."

The Jesse Graham she knew wouldn't have noticed the size of a widow's wood pile, let alone done anything to change it.

He jerked his head toward his ma's house, now a short

ways behind her. "I was on my way home. But if you'd allow it, I'll walk you home first."

She wanted to say no. She meant to say no. She should have said no. But what came out of her mouth was, "If you like."

A smile came slowly to his lips, and he reached out with one hand. "Let me carry that for you."

The basket was empty. She'd taken a loaf of bread and a jar of soup to Felicia Blaine—and she was the one who hadn't noticed the size of the wood pile. Without protest, she allowed him to take the basket.

He turned to stand beside her, and they started toward her grandparents' farm.

After a time of silence, she said, "I heard you're working for Mr. Smith at the newspaper."

"Yeah, I am."

"Do you like working there?"

He chuckled. "Mostly I'm sweeping up. Tidying stacks of old newspapers. Organizing files. But Newton's interesting. The man's got lots of stories to tell. Never knew that about him."

"Were you ever in trouble with him when you were young?"

A cloud crossed his face. Perhaps the memories unsettled him. "Didn't cause any mischief at the newspaper office that I remember. Never threw paint on its windows. Might have stolen eggs from his chicken coop behind his house." He shook his head. "I reckon I stole eggs from just about every coop around town."

"Including ours?"

He met her gaze. "Including yours."

"Jesse?"

"Yeah?"

"Did you . . . did you like me at all?"

He stopped, forcing her to do the same. "Yes, Willow. I liked you. I liked you too much, I think."

"Then why did you leave me like you did?"

A frown furrowed his brow. "You don't know why?"

She shook her head.

"You don't remember how angry your grandpa was when he found us together in the barn? You don't remember what he saw and what he said?" He looked away from her and up at the sky. Perhaps he searched for an answer. Perhaps, if his faith was real, he said a silent prayer. "I'm lucky he didn't shoot me right there and then. I would've deserved it if he had."

"Grandpa wouldn't shoot you. He wouldn't shoot anybody unless they were trying to shoot him or his first. Yes, he was angry with you and me. He'd been angry with us before and you didn't leave town." She started walking again. "I shouldn't have asked. It doesn't matter anyway."

He stopped her with a hand on her shoulder. "It matters, Willow."

She faced him, blinking away unwanted tears.

"That person I was," he said, his voice low, "he wasn't good for you. I didn't have good intentions, and your grandpa knew it. You knew it too, I think, if you're honest with yourself. Yes, I liked you, but there was lust in my heart more than liking. We were headed for the kind of trouble there'd be no getting over. I would've been the ruin of you if I stayed."

Heat rose in her cheeks. What he said was true. That last

night he was in town, she'd wanted to give herself to him because she loved him as only a girl of sixteen can love, and she'd believed giving herself would make him love her too. She'd believed it would make him stay with her forever.

"Willow, me leaving Kings Meadow that night saved you from much worse hurt than whatever you felt after I was gone. It took me years on the road, bumming around from place to place, to figure that out." He took a slow breath and released it. "I've gotta believe God was looking out for both of us when he sent your grandpa to the barn that night. And I'm mighty thankful for it because I've got one less regret weighing me down."

She could almost see it, the weight on his shoulders, and something shifted inside her.

"I hope I came back to Kings Meadow a better man than the one I was when I left. The kind of man who'll do right by others. A servant for the Lord, like your grandpa."

She swallowed the lump that formed in her throat but ignored the tears welling over and streaking her cheeks.

He smiled gently. "I'm sorry. I didn't mean to make you cry."

She shook her head.

"Will you forgive me?"

"For making me cry?" she managed to say.

"For that. For everything, if you can."

She thought for a few moments, testing her heart. Finally, she answered, "Yes, I believe I can."

Strangely enough, she felt a weight come off her own shoulders. And was thankful for it.

6

———

Willow awakened the next morning before first light. She stared at the ceiling, watching as the black of night changed ever so slowly to the grays of dawn, and she smiled, not even knowing why. She simply felt glad.

"Thanks, Lord," she whispered, "for this new day."

She pushed aside the sheet and blanket and rose from the bed. In no time at all, she was dressed, her hair brushed and caught at the nape with a ribbon. Then, on bare feet, she went down the stairs, avoiding the step that squeaked, and went to the kitchen where she added wood to the cook stove.

Her first cup of coffee was ready in time for her to take it outside to watch the sun rise over the mountains. She stood, feet still bare, in the dewy grass, and closed her eyes as the sun bathed her face in light. It was indescribably beautiful, the morning as it came to this valley in the mountains. The trees and grass seemed greener. The sky seemed bluer. The birdsong seemed sweeter.

"Thank You," she whispered for the second time that morning.

Behind her, Grandpa sang in his wonderful tenor voice, "'For the beauty of the earth, / for the glory of the skies, / for the love which from our birth / over and around us lies.'"

She turned toward him and joined her voice to his. "'Lord of all, to thee we raise / this our hymn of grateful praise.'"

"Amen," Grandpa added. He lifted the cup in his hand, a wordless thanks for the coffee she'd made. "Great way to begin the day. With praise to the Almighty."

Smiling, she moved toward him.

"Aren't your feet cold?" he asked.

"Not really."

"Oh, to be young."

"How is Grandma?"

"Still not stirring."

Willow put an arm around his back and leaned her head against his shoulder. "She didn't eat a bite last night."

They stood like that a long while, holding each other with one arm, neither of them saying another word. What was there to say? Grandma was fading. One day soon—perhaps even today—she would step from this world into glory. Their goodbyes would be temporary, but those left behind would hurt all the same.

Tears blurred Willow's vision. "How will we manage without her?"

"One day at a time." He kissed the crown of her head before adding, "'The days of our years are threescore years and ten; and if by reason of strength they be fourscore years, yet is their strength labour and sorrow; for it is soon cut off, and we fly away.'"

"From the psalms?"

"Psalm 90, verse ten."

"Seventy years doesn't seem long enough, Grandpa. Eighty wouldn't either. I don't remember a time when Grandma wasn't with us or somewhere nearby. Even before Craig and I came to live here, all we had to do was run across a couple of fields to see you both. Grandma was usually in the kitchen baking something. She was always telling us stories. And laughing. Nobody laughs like Grandma used to."

"Hold onto those memories, my girl. They are sweet reminders of those we love. But also remember that this world is not our home. Our real home is with the Lord. We are aliens, foreigners in a fallen world." He tightened his hold and kissed the top of her head a second time before letting go. "I'd better see if your grandma is awake."

Willow nodded, a new wave of emotion making it impossible to speak. After watching her grandpa return indoors, she faced the sunrise again.

Threescore years and ten. That's what the Bible said could be expected. A strong person might get eighty years on the earth. Some, of course, went to Jesus long before that. Willow's parents were both only thirty-two years when the influenza took them.

She closed her eyes. "Life is hard, Lord, but You are good. Keep us faithful. Please."

"Willow!"

She spun toward the door, recognizing urgency in Grandpa's voice.

"Fetch Dr. Bunch!"

She didn't ask why. She knew. She sprinted from the yard, not caring that her feet were bare.

Please, God, let me get back in time.

J ESSE WHISTLED THE OPENING BARS OF "A IN'T M ISBEHAVIN'" AS he left home. He didn't need to be at work this early, but he hoped to finish sorting a stack of old flyers before Newton arrived in the office. Jesse thought most of the papers should be discarded, but he would be more successful if he could look at them without the newspaperman watching over his shoulder.

As he approached the corner of Main Street and Valley Road, he saw Willow racing toward him, her skirt flying up, her feet bare, panic written on her face. Before he could call to her, she veered onto the path leading to Dr. Bunch's front door. His heart hitched, and he dreaded what this meant. It must be the reverend's wife. He'd heard from more than one person since his return how poorly she was.

Roberta Foster had been kind to him when he was a kid. No matter how much mischief he'd caused, she'd had a gentle word for him. He'd never felt her judging him, although she'd had a right to. One time, when he was about ten, he'd had a fistfight with Craig Foster. Craig and Willow had been living with their grandparents close to a year by then, and Jesse had said something unkind about their dad. He didn't remember exactly what anymore, but it was something he shouldn't have said. Craig had laid into him, and the two had pummeled each other as best as ten-year-old boys could.

It was Mrs. Foster who'd stopped the fight, and it was Mrs. Foster who'd tended to their scrapes and made certain they'd done no serious damage to each other. Finally, it was Mrs. Foster who'd talked to them about the power of the tongue to either build up or destroy. "You can choose to be good or bad," she'd said, looking from one to the other. "God gave us all free will. You can use that will to do right or wrong or to say right or wrong. But you'll live a better life when you do and say what's right."

Too bad he hadn't listened to her. But maybe he could say or do the right thing now. So he stood in the middle of the road, waiting for Willow and the doctor. He didn't have long to wait.

Willow hadn't seemed to notice him before, but she couldn't miss him when she rushed down the path, Dr. Bunch in her wake. Tears streaked her pretty face. Straw-colored hair had come loose from the blue ribbon tied at her nape. She paused long enough at the open gate to say, "It's Grandma." Then she hurried past him, breaking into a run again, this time headed back to the Foster farm.

The doctor followed in a hurry, but he didn't run. Maybe he wasn't able to run.

"Has Mrs. Foster taken a bad turn?" Jesse asked as he fell into step beside Dr. Bunch.

"Yes."

"Willow looked real upset."

"I imagine it's the end. We've expected it."

"Doesn't make it easier, even when expected."

The doctor glanced over at him. "No, it doesn't."

"If it's okay, I'll come along. See if I can be of any use."

"You can pray for them. Not much else to be done, I expect."

Jesse would do just that. The flyers at the newspaper office could be sorted another time.

KINSEY CRADLED ROBERTA'S HAND—WRINKLED, GNARLED, AND frail—fearing that if he held on too tightly, he would crush the bones as easily as one could crush a baby bird.

Fifty-one years. For fifty-one years Kinsey had slept beside this woman at night and lived beside her in the day. They had starved together and thrived together. They'd known great happiness and great sorrow. They'd raised a son together, and they'd seen both son and daughter-in-law die long before their time. He knew the sound of Roberta's voice better than he knew his own. They'd known each other when they were young and strong and believed they could conquer the world. They'd known each other as their bodies had weakened and failed them. They'd read their Bibles together, and they'd prayed together. Iron had sharpened iron.

"My love," he whispered, leaning close to her still form on the bed, "today you will be with Him in paradise." Silently, he recalled the Apostle Paul's words: *"For to me to live is Christ, and to die is gain. But if I live in the flesh, this is the fruit of my labour: yet what I shall choose I wot not. For I am in a strait betwixt two, having a desire to depart, and to be with Christ; which is far better."*

The sound of the screened door closing told him his

granddaughter had returned, and he blinked back unwelcome tears.

"Grandpa?"

"She is with us still."

Willow went to the other side of the bed, knelt on the floor, and took hold of her grandma's other hand. "Dr. Bunch will be here directly."

Kinsey nodded, but he knew there was nothing the physician could do for his beloved bride. The number of her days had been written in the book in heaven, and she'd reached that number.

"I love you, Grandma," Willow whispered.

He looked from his wife's face to his granddaughter's. They would be lonely without Roberta, but God would see them through this valley of the shadow of death. The Lord was ever faithful.

The sound of another closing door told him the doctor had arrived. As if she'd heard it too, Roberta opened her eyes. She rolled her head on the pillow, looking first at Willow.

"I love you, Grandma," Willow said again, louder this time. Tears streaked her cheeks.

"And I love you." Roberta's response was whispery thin. Hardly audible. And yet very sure.

"I don't want you to go, Grandma."

A fleeting smile curved his wife's mouth and was gone. Then she rolled her head toward him. Strange, how when he looked at her he saw the young, beautiful bride she'd been on their wedding day. The changes were there, and yet he saw through them to the beginning.

"My love," he said, his voice breaking.

"God gave us . . . a good life."

"That He did."

She closed her eyes, drew a breath, and released it. And was gone.

The room went still, as if no one could breathe now that Roberta Foster had crossed over. Dr. Bunch came to the side of the bed, felt for a pulse, looked at Kinsey, and shook his head gravely before stepping back again.

From the hall outside the bedroom, a man's voice rose in song, "There's a land that is fairer than day, / And by faith we can see it afar, / for the Father waits over the way / To prepare us a dwelling place there."

Kinsey swallowed the lump in his throat and joined in, "In the sweet by and by, / We shall meet on that beautiful shore."

While the other man kept singing, Kinsey leaned forward, pressed his forehead against his wife's shoulder, and wept.

7

———

Just about the entire town, plus folks from the surrounding valleys and mountains, came to pay their respects to Willow's grandma when she was laid to rest two days later. It was a perfect kind of day, puffy white clouds dotting the blue of the sky, the temperature warm but not hot, the air stirred by a gentle breeze.

Standing around the gravesite at the close of the funeral, they sang "In the Sweet By and By," and Willow singled out Jesse's voice from the others. His singing had brought comfort as she'd knelt beside Grandma's bed two days ago and, hearing it now, brought comfort again. She'd never heard him sing before, hadn't known he had a voice almost as lovely as her grandpa's.

When the final Amen had been sung, some folks drifted away while others came to shake Grandpa's hand and offer words of comfort to him and Willow. Most of them would go to the Grange Hall to eat a meal and to share memories of Roberta Foster. Willow looked forward to hearing those stories and dreaded it at the same time because they would make her cry, even if they were funny. And there should be many funny stories. Grandma had loved to make others laugh and was nothing if not mischievous, in the best sense of the word.

Willow and her grandpa were the last to leave the cemetery. As they walked toward the Grange Hall, not another soul in sight, Willow tucked her hand into the crook of Grandpa's arm. "Grandma was loved by so many."

He patted her hand. "Yes, she was."

"I hope she knew it."

"I keep imagining her, standing in the glory of God's presence, and I believe she is so full of joy that what she left behind on earth pales by comparison. Praising the Father, Son, and Spirit is all that matters to her now."

That awful lump returned to Willow's throat, and she couldn't reply.

"The Lord is near to the broken-hearted," Grandpa said softly.

She nodded as they turned the corner onto Church Street. The Grange Hall came into view. Fellow mourners gathered in clumps outside, most of them men. The women, she knew, were inside the hall, setting out the various dishes and casseroles that had been prepared for the occasion. She drew Grandpa to a halt, kissed his cheek, then hurried inside to help. Not because she would be needed, but because another wave of tears threatened.

The moment she entered the large meeting room, Ethel Brubaker came to her side, placing an arm around her waist and drawing her close. "How're you doing, pet?"

"All right."

"Is that an honest answer or just a way to shut me up?"

She forced a tiny smile.

"We all grieve in our own ways and at our own speed. Don't let anybody tell you how to feel or how fast you got to feel it. Hear me?"

She nodded.

"I don't share you and your grandpa's faith, but I'm a mighty good listener. So if you need someone to talk to, my door's open to you. You remember that."

"I will," Willow whispered.

"Good." Ethel released her hold. "Now I'm a firm believer that keeping busy helps just about any situation. So you come with me. I've got some cakes and pies to slice, and you can do the same."

Grateful, Willow nodded before following the older woman to a table at the back of the hall.

THERE WAS SOMETHING ABOUT SHARED GRIEF THAT BROUGHT folks together, and for the first time since Jesse returned to Kings Meadow, he didn't feel as if others watched and waited for him to put a foot wrong. Several of his ma's friends and neighbors even made him feel welcome, a true part of the community.

He sat at a table with Ma, eating the food on his plate while listening to the conversations around him, but his gaze returned again and again to Willow. When he saw her leave the hall by the back door, he rose and followed after her, unable to help himself and not caring if anyone observed him.

He found her standing near the creek that ran behind the Grange Hall, her arms crossed over her middle, as if trying to hold in her emotions. Shadows from the leaves of a river birch played over her face as she stared into space.

"Willow?" He closed the distance between them.

She was slow to turn her head to look at him. Perhaps because she was lost in her own thoughts. Perhaps because she resented his company.

"I'll go away if you want me to." He stopped at the creek's edge, leaving space between them so she wouldn't feel crowded.

Her shoulders rose and fell on a breath, then she looked his way. "It's all right. You can stay."

"Is there anything I can do for you?"

She shook her head.

He stuck his fingers into his trouser pockets, and then, like Willow moments before, he stared into the distance. While he waited, he prayed. For her. For her grandfather. For the town of Kings Meadow.

"I knew she was dying," Willow said at long last, so softly he almost couldn't hear. "And because I've known it for some time, I convinced myself it would hurt less once she was gone." Her voice caught. "It doesn't hurt any less." She began to weep.

Jesse couldn't help himself. He moved close to her and gathered her in his arms. He half-expected her to pull away, but she didn't. So he held her, letting her cry, feeling the moistness of her tears soaking through his shirt. And he prayed some more.

He didn't know how much time passed before she drew back from him, sniffing while swiping at her cheeks with her fingertips. He pulled a handkerchief from his pocket and handed it to her.

"Thank you," she whispered. "I . . . I'm sorry about your shirt."

He glanced down at the wet spot. "It'll dry. The day's warm."

"Jesse."

"Hmm?"

"You *did* come back a different man." She held out the damp handkerchief. "The old Jesse wouldn't have held me while I cried. He would've been impatient and made himself scarce."

"I'm sorry, Willow. I'm sorry that's who I was."

They fell silent for a while, Jesse's thoughts traveling through time, touching on the many moments when he could have made better choices and didn't. If he'd lived a better life back then, maybe he would have the right to hold Willow longer, closer, now. Maybe he'd have the right to kiss her again.

He took a step back, surprised by the thought. Kiss Willow? He'd come back to make amends, to say he was sorry, to gain forgiveness from those he'd wronged. He hadn't come back to rekindle an old romance. Although it hadn't been love on his part. He'd been too selfish to call what he'd felt romance. But Willow? She'd loved him. A young girl's love, maybe, but love all the same. And he hadn't deserved it. Could she learn to trust him enough to bestow it again?

He sensed that she was about to say something, but they were interrupted by Pastor Foster calling her name.

She turned toward the back steps of the hall. "I'm here, Grandpa."

The older man's gaze met with Jesse's. "You all right?" The question was for Willow, not him.

"Yes." She walked away from the creek without a backward glance. "I'm all right."

Jesse stayed where he was, posing Kinsey's question to himself. Was *he* all right? Had he changed as much as he thought he had? Because at that moment, all he wanted was to grab Willow before she could get away, wrap his arms around her, and keep her close.

8

On the following Saturday morning, Willow awakened to a bedroom already bathed in morning light. She sat up with a start, trying to remember the last time she'd slept this late. Not since she was sixteen or seventeen, she would guess, and even then it had been a rare occurrence. She'd been an early riser all her life. "Since birth," her grandma used to say. "You were never a lay-a-bed. Up and at 'em. That's always been you."

Remembering Grandma's words, hearing her beloved voice in her head, brought a sting to her heart. Oh, to hear her grandma speak to her again. But that wouldn't happen. Not until she reached Paradise herself.

Oakley jumped onto the bed and licked Willow's face.

"Why did you let me sleep so late?" She ruffled the dog's ears. "Bad boy," she said with a laugh.

Oakley tried to lick her again, but this time Willow moved too fast for the little dog. Still smiling, she rose from the bed, but before she could begin to prepare for the day,

67

sounds came from outside. A rhythmic pounding. With a sharp bark of warning, Oakley jumped off the bed and raced from the bedroom.

Willow brushed aside the faded cotton curtain covering her window to look outside. At the far end of the pasture that held their three milk cows, she saw Grandpa with Jesse Graham. Grandpa held a wooden post while Jesse drove it into the ground with a post driver, replacing the fence post that had fallen over a few weeks ago.

Lift and drive. Lift and drive. Lift and drive.

Clad in an undershirt that revealed his strong biceps even from this distance, Jesse made swift work of the task. Even after he finished, and the two men began to stretch the barbed wire and wrap it around the new post, she felt the pounding of the post driver in her chest.

Or was it something else she felt?

She washed and dressed, including shoes this time, and brushed her hair, then left the bedroom. A pot of coffee sat on the stove, the aroma drawing her across the kitchen to pour herself a cup before going outside, Oakley at her heels. The dog shot off across the pasture to discover whatever had happened while he was shut in the house.

Grandpa and Jesse stood talking now, Jesse's elbow resting on top of the new post. There was an ease about him that was new. He was comfortable in his surroundings, in his own skin, and with her grandpa. And that knowledge sent a warm sensation spiraling through her. The two men had been at such odds seven years ago. Grandpa had disliked the disreputable Jesse and wanted him to stay as far away from Willow as possible. Jesse had disrespected the older man and mocked his beliefs at every opportunity. The gulf between them had been impossibly wide.

"'Behold,'" she quoted beneath her breath, "'I make all things new.'"

Jesse noticed her and raised a hand in greeting. The men exchanged a few more words, then picked up their tools and ambled in her direction, the sun on their backs and Oakley trotting along beside.

"Look who came over to lend a hand," Grandpa said as they drew closer.

Willow shaded her eyes with her free hand. "That's good of you, Jesse."

"Glad to do it. Ma had no use for me today."

She wondered if that was entirely true. Wouldn't Maud Graham rather keep her son close to her, now that he was back in Kings Meadow? He already spent his weekdays at the Kings Meadow Press.

As if to answer her silent questions, he added, "She's meeting with a group of women this morning at the house. They're doing something with quilts. I would've been under-foot for sure."

Willow laughed, imagining him seated in the sewing circle with his ma, Ethel Brubaker, Harriet Stone, Susan Johnson, and a few others. Personally, she found quilting pure torture and was thankful none of the women pressured her to join them as they once had. Grandma had loved being part of the sewing circle, but Willow would rather be outside in the sunshine and fresh air. Life required that she cook meals, wash and dry dishes, launder clothes and hang them on the line, patch her grandpa's trousers and her own dresses, darn socks, and sweep floors. But when able, put her on a horse and let her gallop through the countryside, the wind on her face.

"Where did you go?" Jesse asked softly.

She blinked herself back to the present and realized Grandpa was no longer with them. She glanced to the right and saw him disappearing into the barn.

Jesse grinned. "Lost in thought, huh?"

She remembered that smile. Oh, what it had done to her insides when she was younger. How tempting it was to let it do the same things to her now.

He motioned with his head. "I told Pastor Foster I'd make repairs to the chicken coop for him. I'd better get to it. Feels like it's gonna be a hot one."

"We've been spoiled by the weather. It was a mild June."

He smiled in response, as if she'd said something truly interesting, then gave a nod, and walked toward the chicken coop.

Willow had her own tasks to accomplish, but she allowed herself a few moments of watching him before she turned and re-entered the house, Oakley close behind.

Jesse worked up a good sweat as he made repairs to the coop that kept the chickens protected from roaming dogs and the occasional coyote. Of course, it never stopped a kid bent on mischief from stealing eggs. Jesse knew all about that.

"Hey, Jesse," Pastor Foster's voice wafted across the backyard.

He looked up from the board he'd just nailed into place.

The older man stood near the corner of the house. "Come inside. Willow's got lunch ready for us, along with a cold glass of tea."

"Sounds good. Be right there."

He gathered the hammer and jar of nails and let himself out of the chicken run. After washing at the pump— including ducking his head under the faucet— he gave his hair a good shake and rubbed it with a towel, then put on the cotton shirt he'd removed earlier in the day, making himself slightly more presentable for a place at the pastor's table. At the back door, he paused on the stoop and peered through the screen. Pastor Foster sat at the small kitchen table, and Willow stood at the stove, her back to the door. Jesse rapped on the jamb.

"Come in," the pastor said without looking his way.

Jesse stepped into the kitchen, reaching behind him as he did so to ease the screened door shut.

Pastor Foster motioned him toward the table. "When we've eaten, I'll head over to the church to finish preparing my sermon for tomorrow. But lest I leave in a hurry, I need you to know how much I appreciate the help you've given me today. A lot has been put off these last few months."

Jesse knew without asking that repairs around the farm had been less important for the older man than spending time with his dying wife. "I was glad to do what I could." He settled onto the chair opposite the pastor. "Be happy to do whatever I can." His gaze shifted to Willow at the stove as she ladled soup into bowls. "Saturdays are mostly my own. I'll come again next week. I'll come as long as you need me." Truth was, he hoped there were plenty more repairs needed on the Foster farm because it meant he would see more of Willow.

She brought the soup bowls to the table then, setting one in front of her grandpa and the other in front of Jesse. The faint grassy aroma of celery combined with a hint of cooked onion and a subtle dairy sweetness rose in a cloud to his nostrils, making his mouth water and his stomach growl. From the wisp of a smile that curved Willow's lips, she heard the sound.

She turned away, and he watched her cross the kitchen, the hem of her skirt swishing gently around her calves. Her dog followed her, nose turned high in the air, obviously hopeful a scrap of food would fall his way.

"No, Oakley," Willow said softly as she looked down at him. "Not now."

Jesse's chest tightened. Was it possible Willow had grown even more beautiful in recent days. She'd always been pretty, but today he felt breathless just looking at her.

She returned to the table with a plate of sandwiches. If he wasn't mistaken, that was peanut butter and mayonnaise spread between the slices of white bread. He'd eaten plenty of such sandwiches in the last few years. The inexpensive ingredients were calorie dense and rich in protein. Funny, he'd never cared much for the combination, but knowing Willow had made the sandwiches made them much more appealing.

She placed the plate on the table between the two men. As soon as she sat with them, Pastor Foster closed his eyes and thanked God for His bounty. Then they ate.

No one spoke during the meal. Jesse wasn't sure if that was normal for this family or if it was because he was present. Or maybe they were simply still too grief-stricken to make conversation. He suspected the latter and wished he could find something to say that would ease their pain.

Oakley sidled over from near Willow's chair and pressed his muzzle against Jesse's leg. The dog whined as he turned doleful eyes upward. Jesse bent down and whispered, "I don't think you're supposed to beg at the table, fella."

"No, he is not," Willow said, voice stern.

Jesse glanced up and saw the smile she tried to hide. If he could, he would lean toward her and kiss those lips. But, of course, he could not.

He forced himself to take the last bite of his sandwich, emotion tugging at his heart. He wanted Willow to see him as he was now, not as he'd once been. He wanted her to care for him again, but care for him as a woman and not as a girl. And—he realized with a jolt—he wanted her caring to grow into a lasting love. The kind the pastor and Mrs. Foster had known, even at the end of her life.

Lord God Almighty, do I want too much?

9

The month of July came into the mountains of Idaho like a blast from a furnace. Every living thing wilted in the heat of the afternoons, and every living thing waited impatiently for the cool that would arrive after the setting of the sun.

Because of the high temperatures, Kinsey was all the more grateful for Jesse Graham's help around the farm. After that first Saturday, Jesse came by the farm every evening to milk the cows, and wherever he spied something that needed repair, he was quick to make those repairs without fuss or fanfare. And from what Kinsey heard, the Fosters weren't the only ones to benefit from Jesse's good deeds. Despite the hours he worked at the newspaper office, the young man offered help wherever he could and never expected recompense. However, Jesse lingered longer at the Foster farm, always ready for a conversation with Willow. And it didn't escape Kinsey's attention that his grand-daughter was equally ready to spend time with Jesse.

The morning of the Fourth of July dawned with a cloudless sky and the promise of another hot day. Not that it would spoil the planned events. The citizens of Kings Meadow celebrated this holiday with enthusiasm every year, perhaps because it provided a welcome reprieve from the hardships of life. This celebration would be the same. There would be food and plenty of it. There would be a parade. Nothing too long or too fancy, but folks always seemed to enjoy it. And finally, when night fell, there would be fireworks. Even with funds in short supply, the town would manage to have fireworks.

Kinsey was still eating his breakfast when Willow wrapped her arms around a basket filled with jars of sweet lemonade that she'd stayed up late last night making.

She turned toward the door. "I'm off, Grandpa."

"Already?"

"I need to help get tables ready, and we've got the booths to finish setting up for the fundraiser."

"And what are you selling?" Of course, he knew the answer before it came.

"Lemonade." She held the basket a little higher.

"At least there's plenty of ice from the ice house to keep it cool."

She smiled. "I know. I checked."

"Well, you go on then. I'll join you and the others as soon as I'm done with my morning chores."

After the screened door closed behind her, Kinsey ate the last few bites of biscuit covered in sausage gravy, then rose and carried his plate, coffee cup, and fork to the sink. As he washed and dried them, he prayed for the day ahead, especially that it would be a day free of contention. Trusting the Lord's will would prevail, he headed outside to do his chores.

With Ma's hand tucked in the crook of his arm, Jesse strolled down Main Street. Red, white, and blue bunting draped the storefronts on both sides of the street, and children darted about, waving tiny flags, shouting and laughing. The scent of grilled meats and fresh-baked pies drifted to them from the barbecue pit in the park, mingling with the voices of townsfolk as they visited while waiting for the parade to begin.

Jesse had been present for many Independence Day celebrations in Kings Meadow, but this time was different. He was different. Once he'd been like those kids, running around, playing tag and other games. As he'd grown older, he'd spent more time away from the crowd, instead drinking stolen whiskey and getting into fights. But since his return, he'd slowly become a part of the community. This was his town. These were his neighbors, people he hoped to call friends.

"Morning, Jesse," Newton called from in front of the newspaper office. "Morning, Maud."

Ma smiled. "Good morning, Newton. It's a perfect day for our parade."

The newspaperman looked up at the sky. "No rain like we had last year."

"Thank the good Lord," Ma answered. "That did make for a miserable time of it."

Something told Jesse they'd found the place to watch the parade. So he guided Ma onto the boardwalk, positioning her between himself and Newton.

"Hello, Jesse," came a voice from behind him. A familiar voice that caused his pulse to quicken.

He turned. "Morning, Willow."

She wore a crisp white dress dotted with tiny blue flowers and a red ribbon in her golden hair. If she'd ever looked prettier, he didn't know when it was.

He said, "I heard you've got fresh lemonade for sale at one of the booths."

"We do. Lemonade and cookies. Quilts too."

He turned his head. "Ma, would you like some lemonade? Day's already warming up, and it doesn't look like the parade's gonna start for a while yet."

His ma's gaze took in not just Jesse but Willow too. "Yes, I think I would like that. Bring one for Newton too, if you don't mind."

"I'll do it." He faced Willow once more. "Care to show the way?"

She answered with the whisper of a smile.

He didn't need to be shown the way, of course. The Fourth of July celebration was always the same. Kings Meadow had a small park with a brick and stone barbecue pit on the east end. The booths were always set up on the north side of the park and the tables where people could sit to eat were always on the west side. Nothing had varied even once since he was a kid. He didn't imagine it would be any different today.

They walked slowly in the direction of the park, neither

of them speaking. Not that Jesse didn't want to say something. He simply felt tongue-tied. Odd. He hadn't been shy of speaking his mind when he was with her at the farm. Maybe it was different because he felt the gazes of others on them. Or maybe it was different because he knew she thought better of him today than she had when he first returned to Kings Meadow. And he'd started wanting something more from her than forgiveness.

"Well, well. I heard tell you got religion and now you're the preacher's new golden boy. Guess the rumors must be true."

Jesse stopped walking, causing Willow to do the same.

Ben Travers stumbled out of the shadows between two buildings, a tin cup in his hand. His shirt was rumpled, and the smell of rotgut clung to him. "And look at that. Seems you're back with your holier-than-thou sweetheart. Have you got into her skirts yet? You tried hard enough before. Did you manage it? I'll bet you did. You were always a smooth operator, and she hankered for you."

A soft gasp slipped from Willow's lips. Jesse stiffened. Somehow he managed to keep his tone even. "You shouldn't say such things, Ben. Apologize to the lady."

"I'll say what I like to whoever I like. And I don't apologize for speakin' the truth." Ben swayed as he took another swig of liquor. After lowering the cup, he looked at Willow. "You always had a soft spot for him, no matter what he did, but you wouldn't have nothin' to do with me after he was gone. Thought you were too good for me, didn't you? Well, you're not. I know what you are 'cause I know what he is."

Jesse's hands curled into fists at his sides. He wanted to

punch Ben in the face, and the old Jesse would have done that in a heartbeat.

Willow slipped her hand into the crook of his left arm. "Come on, Jesse. There's no talking to him when he's like this."

"Yeah, that's right," Ben slurred in reply. "You go on with her. Let her tell you what to do. Just remember. I know who you *really* are. I know everything you ever did. You're no saint, Jesse Graham. I'm onto you. A leopard don't change his spots." He lifted his cup, as if in a toast, then stumbled his way across the street and disappeared from view behind the old tavern.

"I'm sorry about that, Willow. Real sorry."

She looked up at him. Did she wonder if Ben was right about him? Did she believe a leopard couldn't change his spots? Did she wish she could let go of his arm and hurry away? He wouldn't blame her if she did. Because right then, he wanted to go after Ben and beat him to a bloody pulp, and he was certain that wasn't what the Lord would have him do.

Was it despair Willow saw in Jesse's expression? Anger? Or a loss of hope? She wasn't sure. But it made her forget the embarrassment Ben's words had caused. "Let's get that lemonade," she said softly.

"I'm sorry" he repeated. "Truly sorry."

"I know. You already told me you're sorry. More than once. And I've forgiven you. Besides, Ben is drunk. It doesn't matter what he said, and it wasn't your fault he said it."

"You're wrong. I still need to say I'm sorry. If I'd been a better person, he couldn't have said what he did to you. If I'd been a better person . . ." He let his words drift into silence.

Tears rose suddenly in her eyes, but she blinked them back as she lifted her chin and straightened her shoulders. If people talked about her and Jesse, they were going to say good things. The gossip of the past—no matter how rightly deserved—had nothing to do with today. Jesse was different now and so was she.

He took a step back from her. "Maybe you should stay here. You don't want to miss the parade. I'll go get the lemonade for Ma and Mr. Smith."

Strange. His turning away hurt more than Ben's insults.

She faced the street again, thankful when it appeared no other townsfolk were close enough to have overheard the altercation with Ben. No one even looked in her direction. Their attention was focused on the west end of Main Street where the first of the floats—a two-wheeled trap, decorated with flags and bunting and pulled by a bad-tempered pony that belonged to Chester Lincoln—was ready to begin its trip through town.

She blinked again, clearing her vision in time to see her grandpa striding down the boardwalk in her direction.

"There you are," he said as he drew closer.

She forced a smile. "You're just in time, Grandpa. The parade is about to begin."

"Good. Good." He put an arm around her shoulders.

Maybe she'd been wrong. Maybe someone had seen what happened. Maybe he'd heard, too.

The Kings Meadow Independence Day parade consisted of three more floats, several children on bicycles decorated with red, white, and blue bunting with flags waving, a dog pulling a wagon carrying the year-old Parker twins, both of them wailing loudly, and a few locals dressed up like founding fathers. There was even a marching band, of sorts. George Leonard kept rhythm on a drum while Arnold Hirsch played his tuba, Ian Stone his trombone, and Lettie Hoover her clarinet. By the time the end of the parade passed by Willow, she was well in control of her emotions.

Along with the rest of the townsfolk on Main Street, she and Grandpa headed for the park, drawn by the mouth-watering aromas rising from the barbecue pit. She didn't admit to herself that she was searching for another glimpse of Jesse until her gaze found him near the grill. She saw him wipe his brow on his sleeve, the heat of the day no doubt amplified by the roaring fire in the brick and stone pit. Afterward he turned a rack of pork ribs with a pair of long-handled tongs. John Leonard, ninety years old and one of the most respected men in the valley, said something to Jesse, and both of them laughed, the sound carrying across the park to where Willow stood.

Emotions pricked her heart. Jesse looked as if he belonged. Really belonged. Like he was one of them. He'd never been one of them before. He'd always been an outsider, rebellious and carrying a chip on his shoulder. No wonder he'd left town without a backward glance. He hadn't wanted to be there in the first place.

"Hey, pastor!" a male voice called.

Willow and her grandpa both turned to see several men standing at one end of the horseshoe pit, two of them with horseshoes in hand.

"Come and join us." George Leonard, John Leonard's

son, motioned to her grandpa. "I've got a dime says I can beat you."

"You know I don't hold with gambling." Grandpa gave Willow's arm a squeeze, then strode away from her. Kinsey Foster might not be a gambler, but he loved a challenge.

She smiled to herself, memories of her grandparents at past town celebrations filling her head. Grandma serving up large slices of berry pies. Folks exclaiming over the taste of her special barbecue sauce. Grandma cheering on Grandpa as he played horseshoes and teasing him when he joined his grandson, Craig, and other boys about a third his age in a game of baseball. Oh, how she missed the grandma of her memories. And it saddened her that her brother hadn't been allowed leave to attend the funeral. Yet neither the missing nor the sadness pressed down on her in the same way today as they had before. She could smile at her memories and be glad for all the love she'd known.

"How you holding up, child?"

She turned again to find Jesse's ma standing beside her. "I'm okay, Mrs. Graham. Thanks for asking."

"There's joy in the memories, isn't there?"

She nodded, her smile bittersweet. "There is."

"Your grandma was a good friend to me. I'm blessed to have known her."

She nodded again.

"And pay no mind to that Travers boy. He's an ignorant fool."

Willow winced. That confirmed it. Others *had* heard or seen or both—and more people than simply her grandpa. Or maybe Jesse had told his mother what had happened.

"You know," Maud continued, "when I was young—younger than you even—I was a handful. My parents despaired of me, especially my ma. I always figured she would think, if she'd lived long enough to see her one and only grandson, that I got my comeuppance when the Lord gave me Jesse to raise. He was a handful too, as you well know."

"Yes, ma'am."

Maud looked toward the heavens. "The good book says we're to train up a child in the way he should go, and that's surely what I tried to do. I tried to raise Jesse right. Tried to teach him good things." She returned her gaze to Willow. "But I reckon God gives us children so they can teach us a thing or two, too. One thing Jesse taught me was to not be so quick to judge or think I know it all. Not even when it came to my son. We can't always know the path the Lord's got 'em on."

"No, ma'am."

"Willow, you look at your Bible and you'll see God used real people who had real problems throughout His story of redemption. He still uses real people. He uses broken people and calls them blessed. He uses faithful people, even ones who fall into sin like King David did. The Lord brings beauty from ashes time and again. I've seen it for myself. I've seen it in my boy, and I think maybe you've seen it too since he came back."

Willow looked toward the barbecue pit, to Jesse as he turned more ribs on the grill and laughed with other men who stood nearby. She appreciated that he was at ease with those men. But did he completely accept that God had raised him from the ashes of his past? Or was he still trying to earn the Father's love, if not His forgiveness?

"I could love him, Lord," she whispered. "Real and true love."

"What's that, child?"

"Nothing, Mrs. Graham. I was just thinking."

10

J esse sat at the table the next morning, feeling bone-tired after too little sleep.

"You got in mighty late," Ma said as she set a plate of flapjacks and sausage in front of him.

"Yeah. I helped with the cleanup after the fireworks." He spread butter on the flapjacks.

"I'm sure it was appreciated," she added.

As he poured maple syrup—a luxury—onto the stack of pancakes, he supposed Ma remembered the many nights he'd stayed out late but hadn't been helping others in the community. Too many ill-spent nights, as it turned out.

She sat opposite him, her expression grave. "I saw what happened with that Travers boy before the parade."

He took a breath and released it, eyes now closed. "Yeah."

"Didn't hear what he said. Didn't need to. I can imagine."

"I deserved what he said. But Willow didn't."

Ma *tsked*. "Ben's a lost soul."

"Like I was."

"Like we all are without Jesus in our lives."

Jesse leaned back in his chair, the breakfast forgotten. "My friend Paul told me once that the consequences of what we've done don't always end when God forgives. He said sometimes we have to live with those consequences. Maybe for the rest of our lives."

"That can be true, son. Sure enough. But God redeems the past even when there are consequences. Sometimes we don't understand that until long after."

"If I'd never treated Willow the way I did, if I'd never bragged to Ben about . . . about her . . ." He raked fingers through his hair. "There were things I said back then that weren't true. How come she's got to pay for the wrongs I did?"

"She made choices too, Jesse. She was young and foolish, true enough. But she still made her choices. And we all live in the same fallen world."

"I can never make what I did right." He leaned forward again, now resting his forearms on the table, one on each side of the plate of food.

"Is that why you stayed far away from her after your run-in with Ben yesterday?"

He met his ma's gaze, silence his answer.

"You don't feel like you're good enough for her, do you?"

"Because I'm not."

"You know what I told Willow? I told her God uses broken people. Always has. Always will. Aren't any of us good enough, but He loves us and uses us anyway, broken as we are."

"If you'd seen her face when Ben said what he did."

"I saw it. Even from where I was standing, I saw it. But I

also saw the way she looked at you later. That girl's ready to love the man you've become far more than she ever loved the boy you once were."

"I came back to take care of you and make amends. I never thought about . . . love. I didn't want, didn't expect . . ." He let his words trail off.

"Maybe you should think about it. It was God's love that got hold of you and brought you back. Love's at the root of everything the Lord does. Ought to be at the root of everything we do too."

He thought of Willow as she'd looked yesterday in that white dress dotted with blue flowers. Pretty and delicate and kind and hopeful. And strong too. Strong enough to take Ben's abusive remarks. Could he be worthy of her love? He'd wanted her forgiveness, but that didn't seem to be enough any longer. Could he ever be good enough to ask her for more than that?

* * *

GRANDPA RUBBED HIS UPPER RIGHT ARM WITH HIS LEFT HAND as he entered the kitchen. When he saw Willow watching him, he offered a rueful smile. "I may have played one too many games of horseshoes yesterday."

"How many did you win?"

"Better than sixty percent." He sat at the table.

"Did you beat George Leonard?"

Grandpa's grin widened. "Three out of four."

"Good for you." Willow delivered his breakfast, then sat opposite him and waited for him to say grace.

After the Amen, he opened his eyes to look at her. "You're not eating?"

"I'm still full from yesterday."

He chuckled. "Wish I could say the same." He lifted a slice of bacon from the plate and took a bite. "But I can't." Casually, he broke off a piece of the breakfast meat and tossed it to Oakley.

"Grandpa!"

He laughed. "Couldn't help myself. Look at those eyes."

Willow shook her head, feeling strangely happy. Loving her Grandpa. Loving her home. Loving her life. With the exception of the insults hurled at her and Jesse by Ben Travers, the Independence Day celebration had been a day full of friends, sweet memories, and good food. Even Jesse's self-enforced distance hadn't marred her enjoyment, perhaps because she was determined to change the way he saw himself and, therefore, the way he saw her.

"Grandpa?"

"Hmm?" He set the fork on his empty plate.

"Shouldn't guilt disappear after someone's been forgiven?"

His expression sobered. "That's quite a question."

She didn't reply. Simply waited.

He slid the plate back from the edge of the table. After a lengthy silence, he said, "Our emotions and our thought processes are not always as they should be. Especially when someone is new in the faith."

His answer proved that he'd known she meant Jesse when she asked the question.

"There's also a difference between conviction and guilt. Conviction is a positive force. The Holy Spirit convicts us of sin in order to lead us to repentance and change. Guilt, on the other hand, is often a tool of Satan. It's meant to shame us."

"How do we help someone understand the difference?"

His smile was tender, his eyes filled with patience. "Sometimes we can't do anything to bring understanding to someone else. Usually they need to discover the truth as God speaks it into their heart. The best we can do is walk the path along with them, side by side. And pray, of course. We must pray without ceasing."

"I will pray, Grandpa."

He nodded. "I'll pray, too."

Jesse arrived at the Kings Meadow Press just as Newton unlocked the front door. His boss glanced over his shoulder before entering the office. "Morning, Jesse."

"Morning, sir."

"Grand time was had by all yesterday." Newton flicked the switch on the wall, illuminating the electric lights and chasing away the shadows.

"Yes, sir."

"And now it's back to work. We've got a paper to get ready."

"Yes, sir."

Newton moved to his desk, the surface covered in papers as usual. "Care to try your hand at writing an article about it?"

"About the celebration?" Jesse's eyes widened. "Me, sir?"

His boss chuckled. "Maybe we can minimize the sirs, Jesse. It's time you called me Newton."

"Yes, sir. I mean, thanks, Newton."

"About the article."

"I'm not much of a writer."

"I'm guessing you're better than you think. And I'm here to edit the piece. Let's say three to four hundred words."

Jesse wasn't sure what that meant, but it sounded long.

"Describe the parade, including the floats and the costumes. Quote from the mayor's speech. I've got some notes on that I'll give to you. Remind people about the food. You know, the smells and the taste. Find out how much money the ladies' circle raised for their charities. Mention the various contests and games. Think about who the readers are. Your neighbors. The folks you sit beside in church. Write the story for them."

Up until now, Jesse had thought of himself as more of a janitor who'd learned a little about typesetting since being hired. He'd never imagined he might actually write for the newspaper.

As if reading Jesse's thoughts, Newton added, "We're a small paper. Can't have a staff member who isn't ready to write as well as set type and sweep the floors." He punctuated his words with a grin.

It felt good, the trust his boss was showing in him. He hoped he could deliver the desired results.

Newton took a small notebook from his pocket and held it toward Jesse. "Take a look through there, son. See what you can use."

"I'll do it." He accepted the notebook.

"You can use the desk at the back there."

Jesse went to the desk and settled onto the chair that squeaked beneath his weight. The desktop was uncluttered—unlike Newton's—and free of dust and grime, thanks to Jesse's own cleanup efforts. He opened a drawer on the right and pulled out several sheets of paper. Next he retrieved a sharpened pencil. And finally he opened the notebook and began to decipher the left-slanting print he found there.

He'd read no more than a couple of pages when his ma's voice whispered in his memory, *"That girl's ready to love the man you've become far more than she ever loved the boy you once were."*

Jesse had returned to Kings Meadow to set things right, but he hadn't thought about the future beyond supporting Ma and asking others for forgiveness. He'd known he would have to find employment, which he'd done with surprising ease, given the nature of the economy. But he hadn't dared think beyond the first days or weeks.

Again, he heard his ma's voice, *"Maybe you should think about it."*

Think about the future. Think beyond caring for Ma and saying he was sorry for the past. Think about more possibilities than just getting by, one day after another. Maybe even think about love.

11

———

On Saturday morning, before the sun peeked over the eastern mountain range, Kinsey stood in the kitchen doorway and watched his granddaughter gallop her bay mare away from the farm. She hadn't said where she was going, and he hadn't asked. Hadn't needed to ask.

"'I will lift up mine eyes unto the hills,'" he quoted softly. "'From whence cometh my help. My help cometh from the LORD, Which made heaven and earth.'"

He took another sip of coffee from the cup in his hand as he watched Oakley return from the pasture. Once the dog sat before him, Kinsey said, "She knows what she wants. She knows *who* she wants. And the thing that surprises me? I believe it's what God wants too. I never imagined that."

Oakley stood and wagged his short tail rapidly.

Kinsey drew in a slow breath, recognizing the peace that flooded his soul. As he released the air in his lungs, he smiled. "I want it for her too. That's an even bigger surprise. I want it for them both."

95

As if in response to Kinsey's words, Jesse walked into sight. Oakley yipped and ran to greet him.

"Morning, Pastor Foster." He bent low and patted the dog. "Hey, Oakley."

"Morning, Jesse." Kinsey straightened away from the door jamb. "You're here earlier than usual."

"I hoped to talk to Willow before I get started on any chores you've got for me."

"She's not here."

"Not here?"

"Gone for a ride on Dixie."

Jesse turned toward the sunrise.

"If you'd like to catch her, you're welcome to saddle up one of my horses. No chores awaitin' that can't wait a little longer."

The younger man faced him again, a question in his eyes.

Wordlessly, Kinsey communicated his blessing before adding, "She'll be headed up to that spot above the river. Remember where that is?"

"I remember, sir."

"Then get on with you. There's no time like the present."

Kinsey caught sight of Jesse's grin—wide and filled with hope—a second before the young man strode off in the direction of the barn.

WILLOW'S MARE, DIXIE, DIDN'T NEED ANY GUIDANCE AS THEY left the valley behind. The pair of them had gone this way countless times before. The familiar trail up the mountainside led to a rocky overlook high above the river that bordered the valley on the south. From the time Willow was a girl, she'd come to this place to think and to pray.

She'd done plenty of praying over the past week. Mostly for Jesse. And for herself too. Because she knew that she wasn't falling in love with him for the second time. She'd already fallen. Hard. And if he wasn't willing or able to love her in return, she dreaded the pain that would follow. Instinct told her it would be even worse than before. Because now he was truly a man worth loving—if he could only let himself see the truth of it.

Upon reaching the overlook, she dismounted and walked closer to the edge where she settled onto a white boulder. The surface of the large rock had been worn smooth by weather and time. Decades and centuries of weather and time. Perhaps God had prepared it just for her and a time such as this.

She sat with her face toward the rising sun, eyes closed. "I'll wait," she whispered. "I'll be right here, Abba."

After a while, her thoughts drifted to the past, to the first time she'd noticed Jesse Graham. Not that she hadn't known him already. He'd grown up in Kings Meadow, same as she had. But when she turned fourteen, she became aware of Jesse in a whole different way. Before that moment he'd been just another bothersome older boy, one who got into trouble all the time. Then came the day when she looked at him and something sparked inside her. She'd realized how good looking he was, the cute way a lock of his dark hair curled on his forehead, the way his biceps looked rock hard beneath the rolled up sleeves of his shirt. A whole year had to pass before he noticed her in return. A year of agony and frustration. Followed by another year of stolen kisses and passionate longings that she'd barely understood. Only her grandpa's unexpected appearance one night had saved her from taking a step too far.

"You and I came up here," came a deep voice from the forest behind her, "that last night. Do you remember?"

She gasped as she shot to her feet. "Jesse?" She whirled to face him.

He dropped the horse's reins and stepped forward. "I was a fool back then. A real fool."

"How did you know I'd be here?"

"Your grandpa told me."

"How did he know?"

A momentary smile curved the corners of his mouth. "He knows you well."

"Why did you follow me here?"

"Because I don't want to be a fool again." He took another step toward her.

She gave her head a slow shake, unsure what she meant by it.

"Willow, I don't want to live in the regret of the past."

"I don't want that either."

"Your forgiveness means a lot to me." He drew even closer. Close enough he could have reached out to touch her. He didn't. "But there's gotta be something more after that."

Her heart raced, and she felt winded.

"I've done a lot of thinking and praying since the Fourth."

"So have I," she answered, her voice barely audible, even to herself.

The way he looked at her with those dark brown eyes,

she felt the gaze all the way down to her toes. Her mouth went dry and her breath became shallow as she looked up at him. At last he lifted a hand and touched her cheek with his fingertips, his caress soft and gentle. She leaned into it, tempted to close her eyes but afraid to break the connection between them.

"These last few weeks," he said, lowering his head until their foreheads touched, "I've realized more and more what I want my life to look like down the road. Maybe it's crazy, Willow, but when I look at the future now, I can only see it with you beside me. I know I didn't treat you right before. But I'm hoping you might give me a chance to prove I'm a different man now."

She drew her head back so their gazes could meet once more. "Jesse Graham, I'm beginning to think you're still a fool. Don't you realize I've already seen the difference in you? Even when I was angry with you, that very first day you came to the farm to say you were sorry. Even then I could see it." Joy welled inside, and she smiled at him. "And when you stood up for me with Ben but didn't hit him like I know you wanted to, then I saw it even more. God got a hold of you right good, Jesse. Right good. And I love the man he's made you. I love you with my whole heart and always will."

THE KISS JESSE GRAHAM SHARED WITH WILLOW FOSTER ON that stone ridge overlooking the river with the sun spilling across the clearing and the pine trees and aspens that surrounded them was unlike any kiss he'd known. Not even with Willow years before. It made his heart want to explode in his chest. It made him want to sing and laugh and shout. He didn't have the right words to use to describe the feelings that spilled through him. Maybe he'd have to open that big dictionary Newton kept at the newspaper office and add more words to his vocabulary.

Willow loved him. This time with a woman's love. A love that wouldn't be shaken. A love that would endure. And he loved her back the same way. A man's love. A *real* man's love.

He pulled back from her, although not far. "What will your grandpa say?" he asked, his voice gravelly with emotion. "About us loving each other."

"He wouldn't have sent you up here if he was against it."

"This'll seem mighty fast for some folks."

A glint shone in her blue eyes. "It took years, Jesse. It wasn't fast at all."

"I haven't had much time to prove myself."

"You're wrong, Jesse. I've been watching. I've seen. Same for others. We've watched when you didn't know it. You weren't putting on a show for anybody. Just living right. And those who haven't seen it yet will see it in time."

Something warm curled in his belly. "I was thinking something else."

"Thinking what?"

"If your grandpa had never threatened to shoot me with his .44 if I didn't get out of town, I never would've traveled the country and finally met Paul. And if I'd never met him, maybe I never would've met Jesus. And if I'd never met Jesus and learned to love reading the Bible, I never would've come back to Kings Meadow and discovered God meant for you and me to be together all along. At least, that's what I'm thinking He meant."

"'The steps of a good man are ordered by the LORD,'" Willow quoted.

Jesse nearly repeated what he'd said so often over the past weeks. That he hadn't been a good person seven years ago. But then he remembered that, apart from Christ, his own righteousness was like filthy rags anyway. And so, he stayed silent, choosing instead to draw Willow close and taste her lips once again.

EPILOGUE

Kings Meadow, Idaho
September 1932

Willow's brother, Craig, was able to get a leave of absence from the Army so he could walk her down the aisle on her wedding day. To Willow's delight, he'd given his approval of the union once he had a chance for a heart-to-heart with Jesse.

Now, as the brother and sister stood in the narthex of the church, Willow's hand tucked into the crook of his arm, Craig asked, "You ready, sis?"

She beamed up at him. "More than ready."

"No doubts?"

"No doubts."

"Didn't think so. You know what Jesse said to me last night?"

She shook her head.

"He said God works in mysterious ways, and one proof of

that was, it took a Bible and a .44 to make him ready to be your husband. When I asked him what he meant, he just smiled and said you would know."

She laughed, joy bubbling up inside of her. The way it had bubbled up so often over the summer as she and Jesse learned to walk the path they hoped to follow together for the rest of their lives.

But before she could say anything to Craig, Susan Johnson played the opening bars of the "Wedding Chorus" on the pump organ, and the doors to the sanctuary opened before them. At the end of the aisle stood Jesse, so tall, handsome, generous, and, best of all, the good man—better than he even knew—who loved her.

God did work in mysterious ways, and she would be forever thankful for it.

A Bible and a .44, indeed.

I HOPE YOU DANCE

ROBIN LEE HATCHER

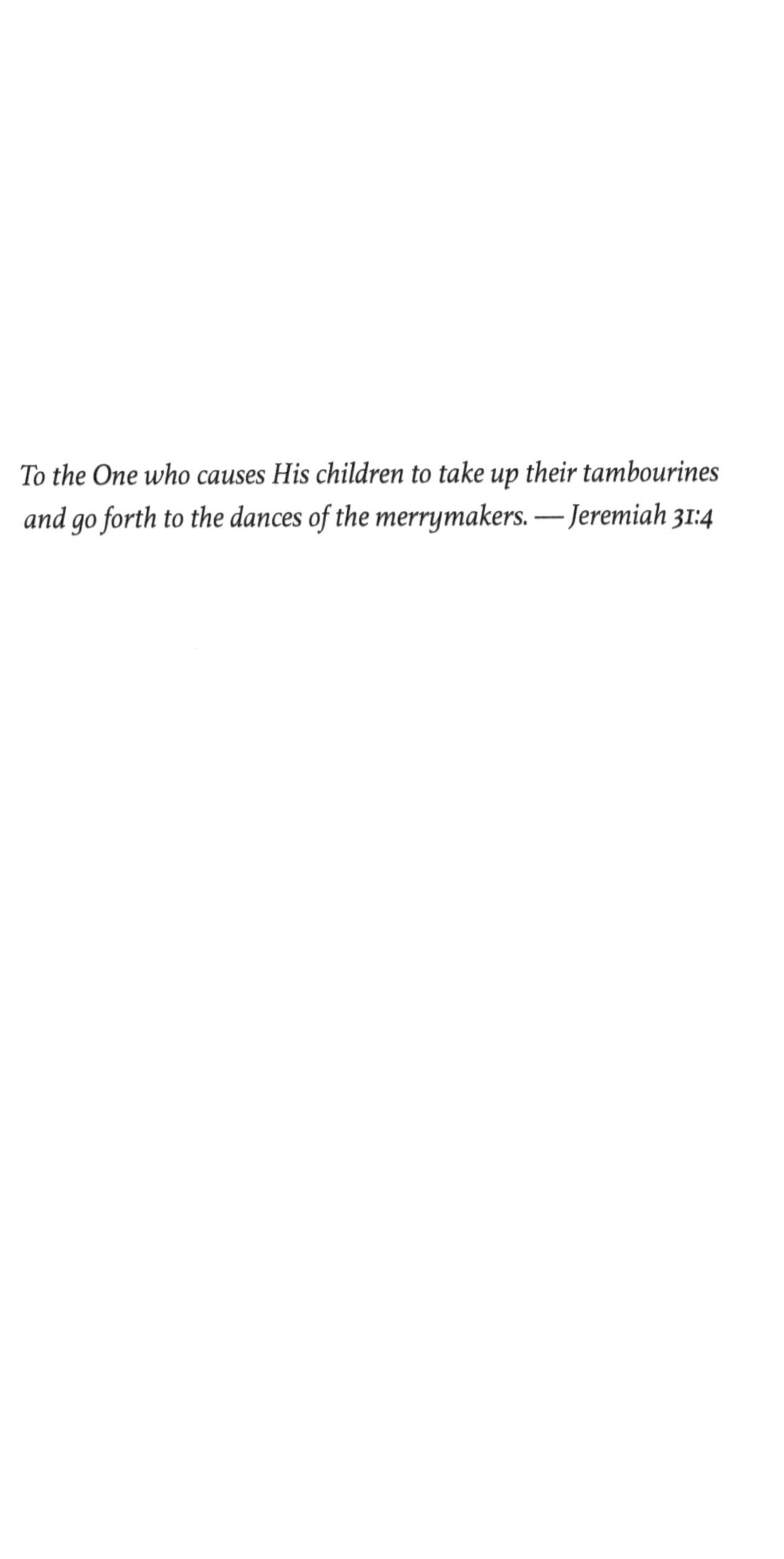

To the One who causes His children to take up their tambourines and go forth to the dances of the merrymakers. — Jeremiah 31:4

1

Kings Meadow, Idaho
June 2015

Summers were made for weddings. Skye Foster had believed that for the past twenty years. Ever since she was six and a guest at a distant cousin's wedding. This July, she would have a small part to play in the wedding of Charity Anderson and Buck Malone. A wedding Skye knew would be the most beautiful and romantic ever held in Kings Meadow.

When she closed her eyes, she could imagine it perfectly. The couple, standing in the gazebo with pastor, bridesmaids, and groomsmen, repeating their vows in the golden glow of an Idaho summer morning. The bride in white satin and lace and the groom in a coat and tails. White folding chairs set up in the park, filled with friends and family. Women dabbing their eyes with tissues. The cutting of the many layered cake. The music. The dancing.

Ah, yes. As far as she was concerned, no wedding was complete without dancing.

She imagined the band playing a romantic country waltz. She imagined herself stepping into the arms of a tall, lanky cowboy, feeling the warmth of his hand as it closed around hers. She imagined moving around the dance floor, the fluttering of her heart in time with their steps.

It was all so romantic.

Taking a deep breath, she tilted her head back and mentally tried to see the face of the cowboy who turned her around the floor with such expertise. But here, at last, her imagination failed her. In her daydream, there was nothing but shadows beneath the brim of his Stetson.

She released a sigh and opened her eyes again. Hard to envision a romance when she didn't even have a boyfriend. At the rate she was going, she would never get to plan a wedding of her own. But that didn't stop her from wishing for it. Only now was not the time.

With another sigh, she set aside the latest issue of *Brides* magazine that had come in the mail, grabbed the keys to her truck, and left the house.

First stop on her agenda was the Clippity Do-Da Hair Salon. It was time for a trim. Her mother, Midge—the owner of the salon—would plead with Skye, as usual, to let her try something different. And Skye would, as usual, refuse her. Long and straight was her style. She liked it and wasn't about to change it.

Next up she had an appointment to meet the vet at the pasture where she kept her two horses, Snickers and Milky Way. Snickers had started limping a few days ago and didn't seem to be improving, even with rest and the use of liniment.

Skye hoped it wasn't serious. The gelding was the best barrel-racing horse she'd ever owned—there'd been five over the years. He'd made her the queen of more than one rodeo by the time she turned twenty. Snickers had more heart than stamina these days, but that didn't matter to Skye. She loved him to pieces.

It took only minutes to drive to the east edge of town. On a Wednesday afternoon, she was able to park on the street right in front of the salon. As she got out of the pickup, high-pitched voices called Skye's name. She looked toward the corner and saw two teenage girls, books in their arms, apparently headed for the library. She knew them, of course, just as she knew almost everyone else in Kings Meadow. Krista and Sharon Malone, daughters of the high school principal.

"Hey!" she called back with a wave of her hand.

The girls moved on out of sight, and Skye pushed open the door to the salon, a tiny bell ringing above her head. The main room—smelling of perm solution and fruity shampoo—was completely empty. No stylists. No customers.

Her mom looked out from the stockroom. "Skye! Is it that time already? Gracious. I thought I would have my inventory done before you got here."

"Where is everybody?"

"Slow day. Lori doesn't work most Wednesdays, and Becca finished with her last client an hour ago, so she went home. When I'm done with you, I'm doing the same thing." She took a cape from a drawer and snapped it in the air, draping it around Skye as soon as she was in the chair. "What are we doing today?"

"Just trim the ends and shape my bangs."

"How much off?" Her mom lifted a segment of hair.

Skye swallowed a smile, knowing what was about to come. "An inch. No more."

"Are you sure?" Her mom placed her fingers, like a pair of scissors, up a good six inches from the ends. "Because I think if we—"

"I don't want short hair, Mom, and you *aren't* going to change my mind."

Her mom met her gaze in the mirror. "Don't you get tired of it always looking the same? You've had the same look since you were twelve, when you wouldn't let me braid it anymore."

"I haven't always had bangs."

Her mom groaned in frustration. "I give up."

Skye laughed. "I wish I believed that."

"Can I at least wash it for you?"

"I'm kinda in a hurry. I've got to meet Dr. Parry at the pasture. He's taking a look at Snickers's leg, and then I have to get home to shower and change and have a bite to eat before it's time for my adult class. I'm teaching them the two-step tonight."

"How many couples have you got coming?" Her mom picked up the scissors and began trimming away the split ends.

"Four couples. They've been a great group. I'm having a lot of fun with them." She drew in a deep breath. "And next week I begin giving private lessons to the Anderson-Malone wedding party members."

"Already?" Her mom's eyes widened as she met Skye's gaze in the mirror again.

"It's less than two months until the wedding. That's hardly any time at all."

"Seems like yesterday when you wondered if Buck Malone might be interested in you."

Skye almost shook her head, but remembered in time to stay still. "That was last summer. Almost a year. Besides, he'd already fallen hard for Charity, so I was way wrong."

"You never minded, did you?"

"Not even a little. And when you see Charity and Buck together, you know they were meant for each other."

Her mom gave her a smile of encouragement. "You'll meet somebody too. You're still young, honey. You've got lots of time."

Skye didn't say so, but she'd begun to feel her biological clock ticking. If she only wanted one or two kids, it wouldn't matter so much, but she had her heart set on a half dozen babies. Minimum. She'd always wanted to be part of a big family. Since her parents had chosen not to give her lots of siblings—only an older brother and sister—she intended to create that large family for herself. With the help of that still elusive husband.

"Close your eyes," her mom said. As soon as Skye obeyed, her mom took the scissors to her bangs, leaving them long but giving them shape. *Snip. Snip. Snip.* "All right. You're done. Hardly worth the time of coming into the salon, far as I can tell."

Skye laughed. "You wouldn't want me cutting my own hair, would you?"

"Heaven forbid! Remember what you did when you were five?"

"Yeah, but like you said, I was *five*." As soon as the cape was off, Skye stood and gave her mother a kiss on the cheek. "Love you, Mom."

"I love you, too, baby girl. I hope Snickers is all right."

"Thanks. I'll let you know."

She stepped outside a few moments later, intent on getting over to the pasture before the vet. So intent was she that she almost mowed down an unexpected passerby on the sidewalk.

"Whoa, there," a deep voice said. Strong hands gripped her upper arms and steadied her.

Skye looked up into the face of a stranger. He was rugged looking with a bit of mischief in his blue-green eyes and one of those I-haven't-shaved-for-a-few-days beards that she liked on cowboys. He wasn't movie-star handsome, but there was something about his looks that made her heart behave erratically.

Who is this guy?

"Sorry, miss." Grant Nichols released his hold on the young woman's arms and took a step back. "Hope I didn't hurt you."

She shook her head, and her straight black hair waved across her narrow shoulders.

"Maybe you can help me. Is there a dance studio around here?"

Her eyes widened. Big, brown, doe-like eyes. "Yes." She pointed. "Around that corner and to the right."

"Thanks."

"But it's closed now."

He almost said a curse word but managed to swallow it. The BC Grant—the Before Christ version—had cursed all the time. Breaking himself of that habit had been tough. It was just one of the reasons he'd kept to himself most of the time since arriving in Kings Meadow. God had delivered him of other bad habits, but the impulse to swear had hung on for dear life for the past four years.

"Maybe I can help you," she added, watching him closely. "I'm the owner of the studio."

Every other thought fled. "You're Skye Foster? Just the gal I'm supposed to see. I'm Grant Nichols. One of Buck Malone's groomsmen. He told me to talk to you about those lessons you're giving the wedding party."

"Oh. Of course. I recognize your name, but we've never actually met. Have we?"

"No, we haven't." *And I'm sure sorry about that.*

"Well, it's nice to meet you now. As for the lessons, they'll start next week. We'll meet every Tuesday night until the wedding."

"That's my first problem. I work on Tuesday nights. Buck thought you and I might be able to work out a different schedule for me."

"I suppose I could do that." She tipped her head slightly to one side. "But if that's your first problem, what's your second?"

"Miss Foster, I've got two left feet."

She laughed.

Man, what a smile. Perhaps he'd been too successful at keeping himself separate from the general population if her smile was what he'd been missing.

"I'm sure that's not true, Mr. Nichols. Anybody can learn to dance."

"Oh, it's true. Ask every girl who's ever had the misfortune to coax me onto a dance floor. They're probably still sporting bruises and broken toes, years later."

She shook her head again. Then she reached into the back pocket of her jeans where she always kept a few of her business cards. "Listen, I have an appointment that I can't be late for. Call me at this number. If I'm not in, leave a message and I'll call you back. And don't worry. We'll find a time that will work, and I'll have you dancing like a pro by the wedding. I love a challenge."

He took the card and read it. *Skye Foster, Two-Step Dance Studio.*

"Please excuse me, Mr. Nichols—"

"Call me Grant."

"Okay, Grant. But I've gotta run. I'll talk to you soon."

She stepped around him and hurried to the silver Toyota Tacoma parked at the curb. She hopped into the cab with no problem, despite looking too petite to drive such a rig. The engine started, and Skye drove away.

Grant stood there for a few moments, feeling winded by the encounter. Then he grinned. He'd dreaded taking the lessons, and only his friendship with Buck had made him agree to it. But suddenly it didn't seem like a terrible idea after all. The weeks until the wedding might turn out to be a whole lot of fun.

2

Skye loved bridal showers almost as much as she loved weddings, and the best part about the shower taking place in half an hour was how surprised the bride would be. Charity Anderson hadn't a clue what was coming.

The two women sat at a table on the patio outside The Friendly Bean coffee shop, sipping lattes from Styrofoam cups. On this Saturday in mid-June, it was sunny and breezy, inviting residents of the valley to be outdoors. Thus, all of the patio seating was taken. Which meant it was difficult to have a private conversation. Other customers kept coming over to their table to say hello and to give their best wishes to Charity. As if none of them had said it to her before today.

When the latest well wishers, Mayor Ollie Abbot and his wife, walked away, Skye repeated the question she'd asked before they'd been interrupted. "So when you get back from your honeymoon, where are you going to live?"

"In Kings Meadow until November. Of course, Buck will be gone a lot in August and September, but it'll be nice for me, being right next door to Mom and Dad. Then in November we'll go down to Boise to stay until early spring." Charity shrugged. "I'm not sure how long we'll do it that way. We may decide to move back to Kings Meadow full time. Did I tell you we converted the back part of the garage of my house in Boise into a workshop for Buck? Demand for his custom-made saddles has really gone up in the last year."

"I'm not surprised," Skye said. "His craftsmanship is amazing. I don't think I could even afford one of his saddles. Good thing I'm not competing this year, or I'd be tempted to go into debt to get one." She made a show of checking her watch. "Do we have time to run over to my place for a minute before we need to be at Sara's?"

Charity nodded. "Sure."

"Great." Skye drank the last of her beverage before standing. "And thanks for coming over here with me. I need to buy a new coffeemaker. Mine's disgusting. Trust me. The coffee is *so* much better here than at my place."

They tossed their empty cups into a nearby receptacle and then crossed the street to where Charity had parked her SUV. As Skye got in on the passenger's side of the Lexus, she wondered what on earth she could say to get Charity to come into her house. She wished she'd figured that out sooner.

It wasn't a long drive from The Friendly Bean to Skye's cute little rental on the hillside. But an idea came to her at the same moment Charity turned onto her street.

"Hey, would you mind coming inside? Just for a sec. I've got this video of a dance I'd like to teach the wedding party, but I'm not sure it will fit in with your other plans."

Charity pulled into the car-length driveway. "Sure. I can come in."

Skye breathed a silent sigh of relief. So far, so good. She got out of the car and glanced up and down the street. No vehicles that didn't belong or made the neighborhood look too busy on a Saturday morning. Even better. Although she did wonder how far away most of the friends had had to park.

She reached into her pocket and pulled out her house key. Not that she would need it. She'd left the door unlocked so the guests could get inside while she and Charity were getting coffee. But she pretended for the bride's sake. She gave the door a little push to open it, then moved back and politely waved for Charity to go in first.

"Thanks."

Charity had made it only one step inside when cries of "Surprise!" filled the air. She looked over her shoulder at Skye, as if she needed an explanation.

Skye grinned. "It's a bridal shower. Surprise!"

When she stepped into the house beside Charity, Skye couldn't believe how many women had managed to squeeze into her small living and dining rooms. Borrowed folding chairs filled every available space between sofa and stuffed chairs. Crepe paper had been draped from wall to wall and over doorways. A sheet cake sat in the center of the table, a punch bowl nearby.

Charity leaned to the side and asked, "Whose idea was this?"

"Mine. Sara's. Your sister's. Half the women here. We all wanted to do a shower, and Terri insisted it be a surprise."

"Terri and her surprises. She's crazy for them."

"Why don't you tell her yourself? She's right over there."

Terri stepped out of the hallway into full view, and Charity's face lit up as she went to hug her sister. Once Terri let go, Charity was passed from person to person, collecting kisses on her cheeks and more warm hugs around the neck.

Skye beamed with pleasure. It was going to be a great bridal shower.

OF ALL OF THE VARIOUS KINDS OF COOKING GRANT DID FOR Leonard Ranch Ultimate Adventures—advertised as "luxury mountain glamping"—his favorites were the cookouts where he was waiting with a great meal when a string of horses and riders rounded a bend in the trail. He loved the surprised looks on the guests' faces, and folks were often impressed by what he accomplished with a fire burned down to the perfect temperature, a good-sized grill grate, and a large, well-seasoned cast-iron skillet.

Magic!

At that moment, the guide, Buck Malone, was helping the greenhorns in his party take care of their mounts so that humans and horses could, as Buck put it, "graze together." Grant turned his attention to the rainbow trout and thin slices of lemon cooking in the skillet. Another minute or two, and the food would be ready. On the edge of the grill grate, a tinfoil container—filled with baby potatoes, red onions, bell peppers, and mushrooms—had reached the perfection stage. Later, the guests would enjoy peach halves and brown sugar that had been grilled together, also in tinfoil. The dessert would be topped with vanilla ice cream that was currently stored with dry ice in one of the coolers.

Grant was thankful for this job, one of two he worked in Kings Meadow during the summer. June through September, whenever Ultimate Adventures had guests—excepting Sundays and Mondays—Grant's days were spent at Chet Leonard's ranch or in the mountains nearby. Several evenings a week, he was also the cook at the Tamarack Grill on the western edge of town. For the past two years, once the Leonards' glamping season ended, the owner of the restaurant, Skeeter Simmons, had increased Grant's hours back to full-time duty. Skeeter had promised to do the same again when October rolled around, and Grant was more than a little grateful for it.

He pulled the skillet away from the fire. "Come and get it!"

After that, Grant was too busy to think of anything beyond the food he'd prepared and the guests he served. It wasn't until an hour and a half later that he was alone once again at the cook site. As he returned supplies to the crates and bins in the back of the Leonard pickup truck, his thoughts wandered to other things.

He'd received a phone call from his older brother last night. Vince still lived in Montana, not far from the ranch where Vince, Grant, and their eight younger brothers and sisters had been raised. Vince had called with the news that his wife, Segunda, was going to have another baby. Their fourth. If there was one thing the Nichols family knew how to do, it was to reproduce like rabbits. At the age of thirty, Grant was already an uncle to fourteen kids—all under the age of eleven—and in addition to Segunda, his youngest brother's wife also had a bun in the oven.

Every time one of his parents or siblings called Grant, the same two questions eventually came up: When was he going to get married? Shouldn't he think about starting a family soon?

No, thanks.

The pressure to marry and have kids was one of the reasons Grant had left Montana. He'd wanted some mileage between himself and the rest of the Nichols clan. He loved his parents and every single one of his siblings, as well as his nieces and nephews. But he had no plans to add to the family numbers. He already felt as if he'd raised a passel of kids. As the second oldest in the family, he'd been called upon to help with his brothers and sisters on a daily basis when they were all still at home. Maybe someday he would find the right woman and decide to get married, but he still wouldn't want any kids of his own.

The right woman.

The memory of Skye Foster popped into his head—and it wasn't for the first time since he'd met the dance instructor. She was a little thing, both in height and weight. A bale of hay probably weighed more than she did. He ought to know. He'd pitched plenty of hay bales when he was a kid on his dad's ranch. But it was her big brown eyes and that bright smile of hers that he remembered most.

With the last of his gear put away, Grant got into the truck cab and started the engine. But he didn't drive away from thoughts of Skye as he headed toward the ranch complex. He had to admit, he was looking forward to seeing her again. He'd be happier, though, if dance lessons weren't part of the bargain. All he could do was hope he wouldn't stomp on her feet too hard or too often or fling her into the wall. Earlier today, Grant had expressed similar concerns to Buck.

"Don't worry," his friend had answered. "Skye's tougher than she looks. She's run half-ton horses around barrels to beat the clock since she was eleven or twelve years old. I imagine she can steer you where she wants you to go." Buck had grinned. "She made a regular twinkle toes out of me."

They'd both laughed hard over that comment.

Grant decided to not worry about it. His first lesson with Skye Foster would be on Monday afternoon. He would know soon enough if there was any hope for him on the dance floor.

Or with Miss Foster.

Charity and her mother, Sophie Anderson, were the last to leave at the end of the bridal shower.

At the door, Charity gave Skye a tight squeeze. "This was so nice of you to do for me," she said softly. As she drew back, she glanced at her mother. "I had no idea you are both such good liars. And Sara too. I didn't suspect a thing."

"I'm glad we fooled you," Skye answered. "I thought for sure I'd give something away before we got here."

"Well, you didn't, and it was great fun." Charity moved through the open doorway onto the front stoop. "See you Tuesday night?"

"Yeah. See you then."

Skye waited to close the door until Sophie's Suburban

and Charity's Lexus disappeared around a corner at the end of the street. Almost at once, exhaustion swept over her. She dropped onto the sofa with a sigh, thankful the other ladies had insisted on helping clean up before they left. The shower had been a great success, which delighted her no end. But what she wanted most now was a nap. She closed her eyes, and visions of white wedding gowns filled her imagination as she drifted off to sleep.

3

Grant had been invited to Sunday dinner with the Leonard family. During the summer, it always felt strange to be at the ranch and not be cooking for the guests of their glamping enterprise. Strange, but nice for a change.

Other than his dad, there wasn't any man Grant admired and respected more than Chet Leonard. Nearly twenty years Grant's senior, Chet had an easygoing way about him, even when life threw him curveballs. He also had a strong work ethic and an even stronger faith. It was the latter that had made him so important as a friend and mentor.

Grant had been a brand-new believer when he'd moved to Kings Meadow. Despite the best efforts of his parents, he'd known next to nothing about the Bible and forgotten whatever he'd learned as a kid in Sunday school. At twenty-six, he'd been partial to beer, cigarettes, swearing a blue streak, and wild women—in no particular order. A lot of his sinful habits had fallen away the night he'd given himself over to God. A lot of them, but not all. He'd still been a rough-around-the-edges Christian when he met Chet. The older man had taken an interest in Grant and had been guiding him ever since.

Now, an hour after polishing off hamburgers, potato salad, baked beans, and cherry-topped cheesecake, the two men were seated on the back deck, shaded from view by huge, decades-old trees. Both of them held open Bibles on their laps.

"I understand what you're saying." Grant leaned forward. "And I love the honesty of the psalmist. But this verse seems to be talking about killing babies. How can that be right in God's sight?"

"The Bible is full of hard sayings, Grant. I believe God wants us to wrestle over the words we don't understand and go to Him for answers." Chet closed his Bible and moved it to a small table. "I also figure some things will remain a mystery or we would have no need for faith."

"And it's impossible to please God without faith," Grant said, feeling a pleasant calm steal over him.

Chet nodded. "Yep."

Grant thought about asking another question, but realized he had his answers for now. Then Chet's attention was drawn to the driveway leading to the highway. Grant's gaze followed, and he saw a silver pickup approaching the ranch complex. He knew that pickup—and his pulse quickened. Unless someone else was driving it, Grant wouldn't have to wait until tomorrow to see Skye Foster.

In unison the two men stood and reached for their hats. By the time the truck began to slow as it approached the barnyard, Chet and Grant had left the deck and rounded the corner of the house.

The driver's side door of the Tacoma opened, and a moment later Skye dropped to the ground. Clad in boots and jeans, her hair covered with a straw cowboy hat, Grant thought her just about the cutest gal he'd ever laid eyes on. She kind of . . . sparkled.

Now there was a word he'd never before used to describe a woman.

Skye grinned when she saw the two men approaching. "Hey, Chet." If she remembered Grant from their meeting outside the hair salon, she didn't greet him by name, although she did nod at him. "Hope I'm not interrupting anything. Kimberly said it was okay for me to come out this afternoon."

"It's fine, Skye." He tipped his head toward Grant. "Have you two met? Skye Foster, Grant Nichols. Grant, Skye."

"Yes, we've met," Skye said. "Hi, Mr. Nichols."

"Just Grant, please. Good to see you." He touched his hat brim in her direction.

Her smile broadened before she looked at Chet again. "I'm thinking about buying another horse. For competitions. I was hoping you might have a good prospect for me."

"You've retired Snickers, I take it."

Grant noticed a flicker of sadness in Skye's eyes.

"Yeah," she answered. "He deserves to take it easier from here on out. He's still got plenty of life in him, but his barrel-racing days are over."

"What about your mare?"

Skye laughed softly, the sadness gone. "Milky Way? Oh, I love her to death, but I'm never going to use her to rodeo. Not if I want to win."

"I've got a few that might be right for you. One in particular." Chet motioned with his head toward the barn, and Skye fell into step beside him as he set off in that direction. Grant stayed where he was, feeling like a fifth wheel.

Chet stopped and looked back. "Coming?"

"Sure." Grant hurried to catch up with them.

To Skye, Chet said, "Grant's got a great eye for horses."

The praise felt good coming from the man Grant respected so much. It felt even better that Chet had said it to Skye Foster. Grant felt a need to impress her. And it wasn't because he liked her looks—which he most definitely did. It was something more than that.

SKYE FELT HER HEART SKIP A BEAT OR TWO WHEN SHE SAW THE blue roan at the far side of the paddock. "Oh, my," she whispered.

Chet Leonard chuckled. "He's young yet. Turned three earlier in the spring. But he's quick. Shows a lot of promise. He's got speed and great confirmation."

Skye had been saving up for several years for another horse. Not that she truly *needed* another. She could retire from competing in rodeos, the same way she'd retired Snickers. After all, she'd taken this summer off and it hadn't killed her. But oh, my. There was something about taking barrels as fast as a great horse could go that couldn't be described with words. It had to be experienced. And once it was, it was hard to say *Never again.*

"Come on." Chet opened the paddock gate. "Let's get a closer look at him."

Skye knew she should ask Chet the selling price for the

gelding. Too much and she would need to look elsewhere. But she wanted that closer look he'd offered, so she kept the question to herself.

As they approached, the horse tossed his head and then trotted across the width of the paddock. He was even more beautiful in motion than he'd been standing still. When he reached the far corner, he spun about and trotted toward Chet and the others.

"Hey, fella." Chet rubbed the gelding's head.

The horse nickered and bobbed his head.

Skye ran her hand over the gelding's coat while walking a slow circle around him. She listened as Chet shared some details. The names of the sire and dam. Date of birth. Training received. It was all important information, but Skye's gut told her everything she needed to know. This guy was meant to be hers. She felt it in her bones. Same way she'd known about Snickers a decade earlier.

"What do you call him?" she asked once she'd made her full circle and now stood looking into the horse's eyes.

"Nana Anna dubbed him River when he was a yearling. Said he's the same blue-gray color of the boulders and rocks that line the rivers up here. The name stuck."

As if knowing the humans were discussing him, River shook his head and snorted.

"He's glorious." Skye rubbed his muzzle.

Chet said, "Thought you'd like him."

"Who wouldn't?"

Grant spoke. "I remember the first time I saw this guy. That same summer when Ms. McKenna named him River. If he'd been for sale back then, I'd've bought him myself. If I could've scraped together the money, that is."

Skye turned, and when her gaze met with Grant's, she felt the strangest connection with him. Because they both liked the blue roan? Or was it something more?

Chet took a long step back from the horse. "I haven't listed him for sale yet. For a while, I thought one of my boys might want him for rodeo events. He's championship material. But they'll both be in college come August and they won't be here to take on the training of a new horse. So now it's time to sell him. I'd just like him to go to someone who knows what they're doing." He looked at Skye. "Somebody like you."

She knew then that Chet was going to offer her an incredible deal for the three-year-old gelding. She wouldn't have to look elsewhere or settle for a horse she didn't like quite as much as this beautiful blue roan. She would want to ride him first, put him through his paces, but she knew in her heart what her answer would be.

"Hey," Grant said. "Skye and River. River and Skye. With those names, I'd say you two were meant to be together."

The thought hadn't occurred to her, but it seemed to confirm everything else she'd been feeling. She smiled at Grant, grateful, as if he'd given her some sort of gift.

But she couldn't begin to describe what the grin he sent back made her feel. It was simply . . . amazing.

4
___

S kye opened the last of the blinds on the front windows of her dance studio, letting in the late-afternoon sunlight, then paused for a moment to capture her hair in a ponytail. Before she moved away, she saw Grant pull up to the curb in his Jeep.

It can't be that time already.

She glanced toward the big clock opposite the wall of mirrors. Grant was fifteen minutes early. She wasn't ready for him yet. Still, it pleased her that he appeared eager to start the lessons, despite his so-called two left feet.

He pushed open the door and stepped inside. When he saw her, he grinned. "I'm early."

She had the same indescribable reaction to his smile that she'd experienced yesterday. "I noticed." She turned and headed for the iHome stereo, needing a little distance so she could think straight again. "You'll have to wait while I get organized. Tell me. What kind of music do you like?"

"Country, mostly. And I listen to a lot of praise music when I'm cooking by myself."

Grant Nichols was an interesting combination, Skye thought as she scrolled through her iPod. He had an eye for horses, according to Chet, and he had the look of a real cowboy. Something more than the clothes he wore. A kind of western inner attitude. He made his living in the kitchen and made no apologies for it as some men would. However, he was ashamed of his dancing abilities. Still, because of his friendship with the groom, he was willing to try to change that.

And how cool is it that he listens to praise music while he works?

She stopped scrolling and selected a Vince Gill album. An extra-slow waltz number was in order for this first lesson, and this album had one that was about seventy beats per minute. Perfect for a novice. When it was ready to play, she turned toward Grant again.

"We're going to start with the country waltz. Ever done it?"

He shook his head. "Not really."

"Okay. Just a few basics. We'll count it out like this: One. Two. Three. Four. Five. Six. One. Two. Three. Four. Five. Six." She went to stand in front of him. "No leaning forward. Keep your own balance. Imagine a string pulling you up from the top of your head." She put her right hand in his left, then positioned his right hand on her back. "Your knees shouldn't be stiff. We want to compress into the floor so that our actions are nice and smooth as we move in a circle."

Confusion filled his eyes. "Compress into the floor? What does that mean?"

"Just keep your knees flexible. You'll get the hang of it."

"What about spins and going backward?"

She smiled, hoping to encourage him. "That's a ways off. All we want right now is to glide. Let's try it without music first. Shall we? I'll count off six, and then we'll begin on the next one. Okay?"

He nodded. His hand tightened on hers. To the point of pain.

"Relax your grip, Grant. You're going to do fine."

He released a humorless laugh.

She counted to six, then, "And one—"

Grant's boot came down hard on her toes.

Ouch! Somehow she managed to only think the word, but she couldn't keep from wincing.

He froze in place. "See. I told you. I'm a lost cause when it comes to dancing."

"Mr. Nichols." Skye showed him her best serious-teacher expression. The one she'd perfected for her elementary school students. "Do you give up so easily on everything you try?"

"What? No. But this is different. I've *tried* this before."

"Not with me you haven't."

Grant opened his mouth as if to say more, then closed it.

Skye smiled at him. "Very good. Let's try again. One. Two. Three . . ."

The lesson didn't end up being the worst experience of Grant's life, although it hadn't ranked up near the top of his best experiences either. He hadn't battered and bruised his teacher. Not to an extreme degree, at any rate. She could still walk to the stereo after the final dance. They could both be thankful for that.

Music off, Skye turned toward him. "That went well."

And she said it with a straight face.

Grant about choked on a laugh. When he recovered, he said, "You're cute when you lie, Skye Foster." As soon as the words were out of his mouth, he regretted them. If he'd insulted her—

Her laughter spilled forth unabated. Not insulted. Amused.

Everything about Skye seemed wonderful to him. Her sense of humor. Her glorious smile. Her boundless energy. Those expressive, big brown eyes. Her luxurious black hair. Sure, he didn't know lots about her yet, but that was the great part. He couldn't wait to learn more. To get to know her better and better.

"Would you have dinner with me, Skye? Tonight at the Tamarack."

Her smile faded by degrees.

His heart felt like it might break in the same way. "Sorry. Maybe you're involved with someone else. I didn't mean to—"

"No," she answered, the word breathy. "There's no one else, Grant. And I'd like to have dinner with you."

Relief rushed through him. "Great. I don't eat out often. I already spend a lot of time at the restaurant, cooking. And it's not much fun to eat out alone."

"I know. I feel the same way."

"Do you?" He couldn't imagine why she would ever have to eat alone. The men of Kings Meadow must all be married, engaged, or blind. That was the only explanation that made sense to him.

"Give me a minute to close things up. Or I can meet you there if you'd rather. My truck's parked in the back."

No way was he leaving the studio without her. "I'll wait for you. We can go in my Jeep, and I'll bring you back afterward."

Grant leaned a shoulder against the wall and watched as she closed the blinds, checked the lock on the back door, and turned off the lights. All of that done, she removed the band that had held her hair in a ponytail, and it tumbled free.

Like an ebony waterfall.

He nearly chuckled at the thought. He wasn't a poetic sort of guy, but Skye seemed to bring it out in him. She made him feel things he'd never felt before.

"Okay." She turned to face him. "I'm ready."

He pushed off the wall. "All right." Outside, he took the key from her hand and poked it into the lock, turning the deadbolt in the door. Then he escorted her to his Jeep and helped her into the passenger's side.

The drive to the Tamarack Grill didn't take much more than five minutes, and since it was still early, the waitress— Cynthia Rogers—offered them their choice of seating.

"Outside?" Grant asked Skye.

She nodded.

"Follow me," Cynthia said with a smile.

The interior of the restaurant had a rugged, western motif. Varnished logs, complete with bark, had been used as supports throughout. The floor was made of large planks of wood, possibly pulled from an old barn. Definitely not the usual hardwood flooring used in homes. Instead of paint-ings, rusty farm utensils, ropes with frayed ends, and antique spurs hung on the walls. Even a couple of pans used in gold mining. There was a bar on the far right side of the large room, but the entire restaurant—inside and out—was smoke free.

When Grant started working at the Tamarack upon his arrival in Kings Meadow, the menu had been heavy with deep-fat fried foods. Little by little, he'd managed to convince the owner to add some more innovative choices. Not that he didn't like a burger and fries himself every now and then.

The outdoor seating overlooked the gurgling creek that ran through town. Trees lined the banks of the stream, their leaves applauding in a light breeze. Plenty of shade made the area pleasant, even on a warm summer's day.

At their table, Grant held out a chair for Skye and then went to the opposite side to take his own seat. He could have sat on either side of her, but he wanted an easy view of his companion while they talked and ate.

"Would either of you care for something from the bar?"

Grant glanced at Skye, who shook her head. "No, thanks."

"Anything besides water?"

He looked at Skye a second time.

"Iced tea," she answered.

"I'll have the same."

Cynthia scribbled on her pad, then grinned at him. "Back in a jiff."

When they were alone again, Skye leaned forward and said in a near whisper, "She likes you."

"Cynthia?" He shook his head. "No. Just friends."

"Hmm."

Now seemed a good time to change the subject. "So tell me about yourself, Skye. Have you always lived in Kings Meadow?"

"Yes. Except for a couple of years when I was at BSU. I didn't go back my junior year." She shrugged. "There wasn't anything I wanted to do except teach dance and race barrels, so I decided to open my studio. I'll go back and get a degree eventually. Just not yet. What about you? What brought you here?"

"Long story. I wanted to leave Montana, and a friend of a friend of a friend told me the Tamarack Grill needed a new cook."

Curiosity filled her eyes. "Why did you want to leave?"

Another long story, one he wished he didn't have to tell. But the truth was the truth. He was stuck with his past. "I was a bit of a hell-raiser in my teens and early twenties. More than a bit, really. Caused my folks all kinds of grief. But when I finally reached the end of my rope—" He paused and looked toward the creek for a moment before continuing. "When I reached the end of my rope, I found Jesus waiting for me there. I was different after I let Him take control, but I wanted to move to a place where not everybody knew what I'd been like before."

SKYE HAD BEEN RAISED BY PARENTS WHO WERE BIBLE-believing Christians, and she'd become one herself at a young age. She was used to talking about God over a meal or at a Bible study. But it wasn't often she met a guy who introduced faith into a conversation this early in a relationship.

Relationship? That might be rushing things. She wasn't sure this could even be called a first date. It had happened so last minute.

"I didn't plan to stay in Kings Meadow for long," Grant continued. "But I liked it here. Right from the start, I liked it. Felt at home. Like it was a place where I could put down roots and change my old ways. I made some good friends, like Buck Malone and Chet Leonard. Men I respect. And now that I'm also working as the lead chef for Ultimate Adventures, I reckon I'll stick around."

"I'm glad."

He grinned. "Thanks."

She hadn't meant to say that out loud, but she couldn't take it back. "Do you still have family in Montana?"

"Do I ever."

"What does that mean?"

"Really want to know?"

She nodded, her curiosity piqued.

"Okay." He held up his left hand in a fist. "My brother Vince is the oldest. I'm next." Up went his index finger, then his middle finger. "We're followed by Martina, Chelsea, Ridley—" He held up his right hand too. "—the twins, Tommy and Tina, then Joshua, Brittany, and finally Heather, the youngest. She's sixteen." All fingers and thumbs were now extended.

"Ten of you? Wow."

"Yeah." He chuckled softly. "'Wow' kind of describes it."

"Anybody made you an uncle yet?"

"I'll say. Fourteen nieces and nephews. The oldest of them is ten. And there are two more on the way."

Skye swallowed a second wow, but she couldn't swallow the envy she felt. "Your family get-togethers must be something."

"You have no idea."

He was right about that. She had no idea what it would be like. Neither of her parents had siblings, and her brother and sister, although both married, seemed in no hurry to give their mother the grandchildren she longed for. There were no large family reunions and never had been because there wasn't a large extended family. Just a small group of five. No, she had no idea what it would be like to have nine siblings and fourteen nieces and nephews. But she would like to know.

Maybe she could find out with Grant.

A yummy, warm feeling spread all through her, and she was afraid she would blush and give away her thoughts.

But Cynthia returned with their iced teas and stayed to take their dinner orders. It gave Skye enough time to pull herself together. After that, their conversation turned to horses, followed throughout the meal by a variety of other topics.

For Skye, getting to know someone had never felt this special.

5

On Wednesday afternoon, Skye hitched the horse trailer to her truck and drove out to the Leonard Ranch. Once there, she presented Chet with a cashier's check that represented every last cent she'd had in savings—and more than a few pennies from her checking account, as well. Then she put a halter on River and led the gelding out of the paddock and into the barnyard.

Before she had a chance to open the back of the trailer, the sound of an approaching vehicle drew her attention around. Her heart skipped a beat or two at the sight of the familiar Jeep. Only then did she realize she'd hoped she would see Grant while she was at the ranch.

She waved at him and smiled. Through the dusty windshield, she saw him grin in return.

He stopped the Jeep a good distance away and hopped out. "This is the day, huh?" He set a hat on his head.

"Yeah. This is it."

"He's a beauty." Grant strode toward her, but he looked at

Chet. "We're done up there until suppertime, boss. I'll head back up at four."

"Sounds good," Chet answered.

Grant's gaze swung back to Skye. "Want some help loading him?"

Skye didn't need help getting this horse or any horse into a trailer. Not even ornery ones. But she said, "Sure. Thanks."

Grant lowered the gate of the trailer to the ground, then stepped out of the way as Skye led River toward the ramp. The horse eyed the trailer with suspicion. She prepared for a refusal. But at the last moment River walked up the ramp as if he'd been getting in and out of trailers every day of his life.

"I should've known that's how you'd be," she said softly, patting the horse's neck.

Grant leaned his shoulder against the back of the trailer and looked inside. "A lot of help I was."

"It was nice of you to offer anyway." She secured River's lead rope, gave the gelding another pat, and then headed out of the trailer.

Grant lifted the gate and latched it closed.

Ask me out again, Skye thought as she stared at his back. *Ask me, please.*

He turned around and smiled that easy smile of his. "How'd the lesson go?"

"The lesson?"

"Last night. With the rest of the wedding party. Any left feet in that group that are as bad as mine?"

"Not quite *that* bad," she said, somehow keeping her expression bland.

"Ouch!"

"I know. Ouch!"

Face toward the heavens, he laughed. It was a great laugh. Full of honest delight. Skye felt pleasure clear down to her toes.

Grant bumped the brim of his hat with his knuckles, pushing it higher on his forehead. "Why don't I ride along with you? Just in case River gives you more trouble getting out than he did going in."

His help wouldn't be needed, and they both knew it. But it pleased Skye that he'd given her an almost plausible excuse for him to join her. Besides, his spontaneity was one of the things she liked about him. Just one of an increasing number of things she liked about him.

"Sure," she answered. "I wouldn't mind a little backup. Just in case."

"Want me to follow in my Jeep so you don't have to bring me back?"

She shook her head. "No. It isn't that far. I'll bring you back."

"Great."

While Grant went to the right, Skye rounded the left corner of the trailer, headed for the cab of her pickup. She stopped when she saw Chet standing not far off, a knowing smile curving his mouth. She'd completely forgotten he was there.

"Looks like you're all set," he said. "I'll get those papers to you by next week."

"Thanks. I'm not worried about them. Whenever it's good for you."

Was she blushing? Her face felt warm. Oh, how she hoped she wasn't blushing.

"Well." Chet's smile grew a little. "Good luck to you and

Grant when you unload the horse."

She gave him a quick nod before opening the door to the cab and climbing in. Grant was already on the passenger's side, but she didn't look in his direction. Her plan was to wait until her embarrassment cooled.

She kept her speed under fifteen miles an hour on the long dirt driveway. No point jostling River around any more than necessary. No point filling the cab with dust either, since both of their windows were open.

When they reached the highway, she stopped and looked both ways. This was a quiet stretch of road, but she never took chances when it came to her horses.

"Clear this way," Grant said as he stared north.

"Thanks."

The road was clear to the south as well. She stepped on the gas and pulled onto the highway.

After a few minutes of silence, Grant said, "Buck told me you put on quite a shindig for Charity last weekend."

"I didn't do all that much."

"Not what I heard."

Simple words that felt like a huge compliment, and her heart fluttered with pleasure. She decided to change the subject. "Is the town where you grew up as small as Kings Meadow?"

"Definitely. A wide spot in the road is more like it. Care to hear how I walked to school through the snow, ten miles and uphill both ways?"

She laughed. "No."

"Shucks. I thought that story might impress you. It worked for my dad and granddad."

"You'll have to try something else to impress me, then."
Like kiss me.

The thought made her go tingly all over. She'd never felt like this about a guy. She'd had boyfriends, of course. But this was different. Did Grant feel it too?

WHAT WAS IT ABOUT BEING IN SKYE'S COMPANY THAT MADE Grant feel like a million bucks? Since meeting her, she'd been his first thought when he awakened in the mornings and his final thought when he fell asleep at night. And ever since their dinner together, he'd thought of her most of the hours between waking and sleeping as well.

His dad had told him once that when Grant met *the* girl, he would know it. At the time Grant hadn't believed there was such a thing as *the* girl. At the time he hadn't thought he'd ever want to settle down with any woman. Why limit himself to one entrée when he could try every choice at the all-you-can-eat buffet?

But once again, the man who'd thought that way was BC Grant. He'd changed, and the way he looked at women had changed. And something about Skye Foster was changing him even more. For the first time in his life, marriage wasn't a remote possibility.

Hold your horses. You hardly know her.

He looked over at Skye as she slowed the truck before turning onto a narrow, winding road that took them closer to the mountains. A few minutes later, she pulled into an area where the wild grasses had been flattened by truck and trailer wheels. Not exactly a parking lot, but the next best thing.

When Skye got out of the truck, a couple of horses in the nearby pasture came trotting toward the wood and barbed-wire fence. Arriving at the gate, the brown-and-white paint nickered a welcome.

"Snickers?" Grant asked as he closed the passenger's door behind him.

"Yes." She went to the gate and stroked the gelding's head. "I've brought you a friend, boy. Think you can show him the ropes?"

The Appaloosa thrust her head over the top of the gate too. Skye moved to the mare and repeated the stroking motions. "You'll be nice to him. Right?"

Grant slipped his iPhone from his shirt pocket. It didn't make calls most anywhere in Kings Meadow—no cellular company thought it worthwhile to invest in this area off the beaten path—but that's not what he wanted it for. The phone had a great camera. He held it out in front of him, pointed it toward Skye and her horses, and snapped several pictures.

She looked at him, smiling. "What are you doing?"

"Taking pictures."

"I know that. But why?"

He strode over to her and held the screen so she could see the last photo. "Because you are in your element."

Her gaze lifted to meet his, but she didn't speak. After a few seconds, her eyes widened and her smile faded.

It was hard not to focus on her mouth, harder still not to lean down and kiss her. He hadn't known her long enough to do that. The old Grant wouldn't have cared that it was too early in their relationship. If he kissed a girl and scared her away, no worries. He would meet someone else soon enough. But the man he was today cared a lot. He wanted to do everything right, and he sure didn't want to risk losing her before he'd had a chance to see where these feelings of his might go.

Clearing his throat, he took a step back. "Shall we get River unloaded?" He returned the iPhone to his pocket.

"Yes. Let's." Her reply had a breathless quality.

For the second time, he had to fight back the urge to kiss her.

Looking at the ground, she hurried past him. Had she sensed his desire? Had he blown it already?

Skye didn't wait for Grant to join her before lowering the gate and stepping into the trailer. River came out with the same ease as he'd entered. The blue roan might be young and have lots of training still ahead of him, but he had intelligence and a calm nature. That boded well for both horse and rider.

Grant went to the pasture gate and unlatched it while Skye led her new gelding toward him. "Snickers," he said. "Milky Way. Get back. Get back now." He slowly swung the gate inward, keeping his eyes on the two horses. But they seemed willing to wait until River was set free before crowding in to inspect him.

Skye led the blue roan several yards beyond the gate before stopping, patting his neck, and saying something Grant couldn't make out. Then she turned the horse loose. He trotted a short distance away. Head high, he whinnied. Snickers replied and walked toward the newcomer. Milky Way held her distance.

"Looks like they're gonna get along fine," Grant said.

Skye glanced in his direction and nodded.

"Do you own this property?"

"No," she answered as she returned to the gate. "I rent it. Dad and Mom used to have some land south of town where we kept our horses when I was growing up. But they had to sell it when the economy took a downturn. That time was hard on a lot of folks around here."

"Your mom's a beautician—"

"Stylist," she interrupted. "If you call Mom a beautician, it makes her feel old."

He grinned at her. "Stylist. Sorry. Definitely don't want to make your mom feel old. She wouldn't like me much. What does your dad do?"

"He teaches history at the junior high school and coaches track-and-field."

"So you're a teacher like your dad?"

Her expression said she was pleased by the comparison he'd made. "Not quite like my dad. He had to get his college degree to do what he does. I just took dance lessons every year from the time I was six until I was seventeen."

"What kind of dance?"

"All kinds. Tap. Ballet. Ballroom. Country. Miss Cooper taught everything." As she spoke, she walked to the back of her truck and began to unhook the trailer. "My dance teacher was really great. I was never going to be a prima ballerina or anything, but she wasn't after perfection from her students. She simply wanted to impart the joy of dance."

"From what I've seen, she succeeded."

Grant stepped forward to help lift the trailer off the hitch. When his hands landed on the bar beside hers, she looked up, a flicker of surprise in her eyes. Surprise and something more. Their heads were close. To kiss her, all he needed to do was sway forward a few inches. But before he could take action, she looked down again. With a strong yank, she freed the trailer from the hitch without his help.

Next time, Miss Foster. Next time I get the chance to kiss you, I'm taking it.

6

———

On the following Saturday, the groom, best man, and four groomsmen—including Grant—climbed into Ken Malone's minivan. They were on their way to be fitted for morning jackets and all the accessories—trousers, shirt, waistcoat, pocket square, and cravat—for the wedding. Grant had been in enough of his siblings' weddings to know what to expect once they got to the men's store in Boise. Although none of their weddings had been quite as formal as the Anderson-Malone wedding would be. Wearing tails would be a first for Grant.

The Malone brothers sat in the front of the automobile, Ken driving and Buck in the passenger's seat. Behind them were Grant and Tom Butler, the Methodist minister. Buck's soon-to-be brother-in-law, Rick Jansen—who'd driven to Kings Meadow from Sun Valley that morning—had the third row of seats to himself. From all appearances, Rick planned to sleep until they reached their destination.

Once on the highway, with Ken and Buck talking baseball, Grant said to Tom, "I guess you don't find yourself serving as a groomsman very often."

"It's a first, actually. I'm enjoying the experience."

"Even the dance lessons?"

Tom chuckled. "Even the dance lessons. But we're all sorry you can't be there the same night as the rest of us."

"It's okay. Skye and I found a time that works for both of us." He schooled his features, trying not to sound overly interested. "She goes to your church, doesn't she?"

"Yes, she does. All the Fosters do. Good family."

Grant nodded as his gaze drifted out the window at the passing terrain. His thoughts drifted too. Back to Kings Meadow. Back to Skye. It had only been three days since he'd gone with her under the pretense of helping unload her new horse, but those three days had seemed extra long.

Why didn't I pick up the phone and call her?

He'd wanted to. It almost scared him how much he'd wanted to. He'd never felt this way before, as if he were headed over a waterfall in a raft, not knowing if he would survive the drop but willing to take the risk because of what he might find at the bottom. Skye liked him. He was fairly certain of that. The last thing he wanted to do was spook her by moving too fast. By coming on too strong.

By kissing her too soon.

Her image filled his mind. Did she *look* like the kind of gal who would spook that easy? The question made him grin.

Not on your life.

ON HER KNEES, SKYE SCRUBBED THE SHOWER GROUT WITH A toothbrush. Attacked it, more like. Frustration had been building in her for the past three days, and she was letting it out with a fit of cleaning.

She'd been certain Grant would call her. But her home phone hadn't rung on Thursday or Friday. It had been just as silent this morning.

Maybe I misread him.

No. No, she hadn't misread Grant. He was attracted to her. Maybe she was a little out of practice. She hadn't had a steady boyfriend in a while. But she hadn't lost her senses completely. She knew when a guy was interested. Grant Nichols was interested.

Maybe he's shy.

No, that didn't make sense either. He wasn't shy around her. Not at all. He was friendly and inquisitive. And when he looked at her—

Pleasure skittered up her spine at the memory.

Skye sat back on her heels, and with the back of her rubber glove she pushed her bangs off her forehead.

"I like him so much," she whispered. Then she straightened, eyes widening. "Maybe he doesn't know I like him."

As if in response, the long-awaited ring of the telephone came to her from the other end of the house. She shot to her feet, yanking off the rubber gloves and dropping them in the sink before rushing out of the bathroom and down the hallway to the kitchen. She grabbed the phone without even taking time to check the caller ID.

"Hello?" She squeezed her eyes closed and held her breath, hoping.

"Hi, Skye."

Disappointment sliced through her at the familiar voice. "Hi, Charity."

"I was wondering. Would it be all right if Mom and Dad joined our group on Tuesday nights? I know they didn't sign up for the lessons. They go dancing all the time as it is. But now Mom says it sounds like we're having too much fun without them."

"Sure. They're welcome to come. Everybody can get better with a few lessons, even if they know what they're doing."

"Terrific. And while I've got you on the phone, can I just say thanks again for the bridal shower? It was so much fun. Buck says the bride's the one who gets to have all the fun." Charity laughed softly. "I gave him a couple of twenties and told him not to party too hard while he and the guys are in Boise."

What guys? Skye pressed the receiver tighter against her ear. "What's he doing in Boise?"

"Today's the day they all get fitted for their morning suits."

"Grant too? I thought he worked on Saturdays."

"Mmm. I guess Chet gave him the day off. I'm glad, 'cause it will be good to mark this off the wedding to-do list."

Skye's entire body seemed to lighten. Grant was with Buck and the other groomsmen. He couldn't or wouldn't call her when he was down in Boise. Of course, that didn't explain away the silence of the phone on Thursday and Friday, but Grant worked two jobs. Perhaps he'd tried to call her when she wasn't in. Some people didn't like to leave messages. Maybe he was one of them.

"Skye? Are you still there?"

"What? Yes. Yes, I'm still here. Something was . . . about to boil over on the stove." She winced as the lie slipped off her tongue. "Sorry."

"Sounds like you're busy. I won't keep you any longer. See you Tuesday."

"See you Tuesday. Bye."

Skye returned the handset to the phone cradle but didn't move away from the kitchen counter. There wasn't much point hanging around the house, waiting for the phone to ring again. Not with Grant in Boise for what sounded like at least several hours.

The grout could wait. She needed some fresh air.

GRANT WASN'T A TUXEDO OR MORNING SUIT KIND OF GUY. BUT he had to admit the party of men looked handsome in gray tailcoats and trousers with accents of lavender.

As he stared at his reflection in the mirror, he wondered if this was the type of wedding Skye Foster would want. Not him. If he ever got married, he would want it to be by a cowboy preacher with the wedding party and guests all on horseback. Maybe have a big barbecue for the reception.

He gave his head a shake, uncomfortable with the direction of his thoughts. He and Skye hadn't even had an official date yet. They were a long ways from romance, and even if romance happened between them, they were still a long ways from talk of a wedding—*if* that time ever came.

"I've got everything I need, Mr. Nichols," the tailor said, holding out his hands toward Grant's shoulders to help remove the jacket.

"Thanks." He shrugged out of the tailcoat, then went into a nearby dressing room. It didn't take long to shed the rest of the wedding finery and get back into jeans, boots, and cotton shirt. Funny, how much more himself he felt with the right clothes on.

When he came out of the dressing room, he found the other men waiting for him.

"Lunch is on Charity," Buck said with a grin. "Where do you want to eat?"

Ken suggested a popular pizza parlor on State Street.

As they headed for the car, Tom said, "Buck, now that it's getting closer, how do you think you'll like living down here?"

"I've gotten used to the idea," Buck answered. "I'm no fan of the traffic, but since both Charity and I will be working out of the home, I guess we can avoid the worst of it. And we'll be back in Kings Meadow from spring until after hunting season."

"Sounds like a good compromise."

"It was an easy one to make, once I realized how much I loved her."

Up to that moment, Grant had only listened with half an ear. But now Buck's remark reminded him of something his brother Vince had said to him some years ago. *"I'd do anything for Segunda. You know. Climb the highest mountain. Swim the deepest sea. Just so long as she agrees to marry me."*

He pictured Skye once again. Would he want to climb the highest mountain and swim the deepest sea for her? He'd been on his own for a long time. He hadn't needed to make any compromises. He'd only had himself to think about. Was he ready to put someone else's needs ahead of his own?

He didn't know the answers, but he intended to figure them out. The sooner, the better.

7

———

Skye glanced at her watch and quickened her pace. She was late for church. Again. The congregation would be singing the opening hymn by now. She would have to slip into the back and hope nobody noticed her tardiness.

Rounding the corner, she looked toward the front doors of the church. Her heart flip-flopped. Grant Nichols stood on the steps. His jeans looked new, his black hat obviously one he kept nice for dress occasions. When he saw her, he came down the steps to await her.

"I thought maybe you weren't coming," he said as she drew near.

"I'm late." As if he didn't know that already.

Voices raised in song drifted through the closed doors.

He grinned, his eyes saying, *You're right. I already knew you were late.*

"What are you doing here?" That sounded rude. "I mean, don't you go to Meadow Fellowship?"

Grant shrugged. "I thought it was about time I heard Tom preach. Mind if I sit with you?"

Oh, the hammering of her heart. Could he hear it above the singing from inside?

"No," she answered in a breathless voice. "I don't mind. But we'd better hurry."

He cupped her elbow with his hand and guided her up the steps, opening the door with his free hand. She slipped into the shadowy narthex, and he followed right behind. Just as they were about to move into the sanctuary, the strains of the amen filled the air.

Skye hurried toward the back pew, hoping to reach it before the congregation sat down, hoping no one would notice how late she was. *How late* we *are*. The thought made her tingle from head to toe.

She stepped into the pew and turned, her gaze sliding to Grant as he moved in at her side. He removed his hat, and when they sat, he placed it on his left knee.

How long had it been, she wondered, since a man had come to church to be with her? Never. Not really. When she was younger, she'd sat with the boys from youth group. Later, she'd often sat with rodeo friends who came to church as a group. But coming to church to be with her? That hadn't happened until now. Of course, Grant had said it was to hear Tom preach, but instinct told her that she was the real reason—and it felt good.

Grant saw her looking at him and smiled. There was that tingling sensation again. She looked toward the pulpit, lest he see what she felt.

Skye had dreamed of marriage, a husband, and lots of children since she was a girl in pigtails. But she'd longed for all of that under God's covering and blessing. Was it beginning to come true at last?

The service passed in a blur. Skye had a difficult time concentrating on the words spoken and the songs sung. She tried to focus, but it seemed an impossible task.

The congregation rose for Tom Butler's closing prayer, and when he said "Amen," the sanctuary buzzed with voices as people began to depart. Friendly invitations to Sunday dinner were spoken. Hugs were given. Laughter erupted from small groups.

"So," Skye said to Grant, "what did you think?"

"I liked it. Tom's a good preacher. Figured he would be." He stepped backward out of the pew, then waited for her to exit and walk with him.

Skye felt warmth color her cheeks. So strange. She didn't blush easily. Why now? Why this? Before she could answer her own questions, her mom's voice intruded.

"Skye, you *are* here."

As her parents approached, Sky answered, "Yes, I was running late, so we sat in the back."

The word *we* drew her mom's gaze to Grant.

"Mom. Dad. This is Grant Nichols. Grant, my parents, Midge and Rand Foster."

The two men shook hands and exchanged a greeting while her mom turned questioning eyes upon Skye. She returned the look with a small shake of the head. A shake that said, *Don't pry.*

"So," her mom said, as if she hadn't understood the silent warning, "what are you two doing for Sunday dinner?" Her gaze took in both Skye and Grant.

Skye wanted to sink into the floor.

Grant didn't look bothered. He answered, "Mrs. Foster, I was planning to ask your daughter to go for a drive. It's a fine summer day. I thought we'd get something to eat up in McCall." He glanced over at Skye. "Interested?"

The embarrassment over her mom's question vanished as she nodded to Grant.

"Well, you two have fun," her mom said. Then she leaned in to kiss Skye's cheek before whispering, "Call me later."

Grant once again cupped Skye's elbow, and they followed her parents out of the church, all of them pausing long enough to speak to Tom Butler before passing through the open doors. On the sidewalk, her mom and dad said good-bye to them and walked toward the church parking lot.

Grant tipped his head in the opposite direction. "I'm parked down thataway. You ready? Do you need to go home first?"

"No. I'm ready."

"Great."

He stepped around to her left side so that he walked closest to the street. Skye wondered if he treated all women with this much care and respect. But as soon as the thought came to her, she knew the answer was yes. He was that kind of man. It was obvious that was how he'd been raised.

She glanced at him, curious to know more about that. "Have your parents come for a visit since you moved to Kings Meadow?"

"Nope. Not yet. You know how hard it is for a rancher to get away for any length of time. Dad takes care of most of the ranch work himself. I've got brothers who pitch in, of course, but they've got other jobs, and all but one have families of their own." He gave a slight shrug. "So I go home for visits when I can."

They arrived at his Jeep, and he held the door for her as she got in. What was it about his polite actions that made her feel pretty and feminine? And so very eager to know what would come next.

Northbound traffic was light on this summer Sunday afternoon, and Grant was content to drive in silence with Skye at his side. The windows were down, and the wind tugged at their hair. The air smelled fresh and sweet. He glanced to his right and saw a smile curve the corners of her mouth.

That's a good sign.

When he had to slow down for a series of curves in the winding road, he said, "I've got a friend who recently opened a restaurant in McCall. I thought we'd eat there. Unless you're too hungry to wait that long."

"I can wait," she answered. "There're not a lot of choices between here and there anyway."

He sensed her gaze upon him. It was insane, the way it made him feel. The way *she* made him feel. And it surprised him how eager he was to dive headlong into the insanity.

"Okay to have some music?" she asked, already reaching for the audio control.

His Jeep was over twenty years old, but he'd had a new stereo system put in the previous year. Even with the windows down, the speakers put forth a great sound. The playlist was a mixture of classic country and hits by current recording artists, and he knew he'd chosen well when Skye began to sing along. Soon Grant's voice joined hers.

The miles seemed to melt away beneath the spinning tires as they sang their way toward their destination. When they tired of singing, they chatted about this and that. Grant always enjoyed learning something new about Skye. And even when they fell silent, it was comfortable instead of awkward. Before Grant knew it, they had reached the outskirts of McCall. He eased off the gas as the speed limit dropped, ten miles per hour at a time. Skye reached over and turned off the stereo.

At last, they entered the resort town. His friend, Andy Davidson, had given Grant clear directions to the restaurant's location. Easy to follow. A right, a left, and another left. After the last turn, at the end of a short road, he saw the sign on a new building: *The Sundown*.

"There it is," he said to Skye.

"Good. I'm famished."

After parking the Jeep, Grant hopped out and hurried around to open the door for Skye. He offered his hand, and she took it without hesitation. As if they'd been holding hands for years. He was sorry when she let go.

"How do you know the owner?" she asked as they walked toward the entrance.

"Andy's from Montana too. We met at the university in our freshman year."

"And you bonded over your common interest in food and cooking?"

Grant chuckled. "No. He was a business major. He planned to be a CEO of one corporation or another by the time he was thirty. But the first business he invested in was a little hole-in-the-wall restaurant, and he found he liked running it. So he bought a place that was bigger and better and liked it even more. Then he inherited this piece of property from a relative and decided to tear down what was on it and build The Sundown."

"I've never heard of it."

"Not surprised." He pulled the restaurant door open and waved her inside. "It just opened a couple of weeks ago."

"Has he tried to steal you from Ultimate Adventures and the Tamarack Grill?"

Before Grant could answer in the affirmative, Andy appeared, walking toward them with an arm outstretched.

"Great to see you." Andy shook Grant's hand with gusto. "Have you thought about my offer?" Without waiting for an answer, Andy looked at Skye. His eyes sparked with appreciation, and his voice deepened as he said, "You must be Miss Foster. A pleasure to meet you. I'm Andy Davidson."

"It's nice to meet you too."

"Was good of you to drag Grant out of Kings Meadow. I've been after him to come up to McCall for months, but he's always busy."

Skye glanced in Grant's direction. "This was all his idea. I had nothing to do with it." She smiled, and the warmth of her gaze made him feel like a hero out of one of his sisters' romance novels.

After a period of silence, Andy cleared his throat. "I've got the best table in the house all ready for the two of you." He motioned for them to follow.

Andy hadn't lied. It was a great table. At the back of the restaurant, up five steps, then up another five, the table looked out over the lake. Sunlight glimmered off the water in sparks of gold and silver. Waves created by breeze and boat motors lapped at the shore below them.

"It's beautiful," Skye said.

Andy grinned at them both and then walked away. Moments later, the waitress came to take their beverage order.

As soon as the waitress was once again out of hearing, Skye leaned toward Grant. "So he *has* tried to steal you away from Kings Meadow," she said in a hushed tone.

He shrugged, liking that she'd overheard Andy's question. Not that he wanted to be prideful, but still ...

"You aren't going to leave, are you?" There was earnest concern in her voice now.

He matched her posture, his gaze holding hers. "I've got a few good reasons not to leave." A slow smile curved his mouth before he added, "At least, I hope so, Skye." Another few heartbeats. "Do I?"

The room seemed to spin. Skye's heart raced. The conversations of other diners dimmed.

"I've got a few good reasons not to leave ... At least, I hope so, Skye ... Do I?"

She found it hard to draw a breath as the words repeated in her head. Was he asking about her? About her feelings? Was she one of those good reasons for him not to leave Kings Meadow?

Before she could think of what to say, the waitress arrived with their beverages. Skye felt a sudden and strong dislike for the girl and her lousy timing. Oblivious, the waitress asked, "Are you ready to order?"

Skye glanced at the menu, settling on the first thing she saw. "I'll have the lemon-crusted chicken."

"Any sides?"

She shook her head. *Hurry up. Go away.*

The waitress looked at Grant.

"I'll have the pan-seared trout, please. Garlic mashed potatoes for the side."

The waitress smiled. "I'll have these right out." She walked away in the direction of the kitchen.

Skye feared the interruption had ruined the mood, but when Grant's gaze returned to her, the intense look in his eyes made her pulse gallop a second time.

He drew his chair closer to hers. "Skye, I've never known anyone like you. Never felt this way before. There's something . . . something special going on here." He pointed to himself, then to her. "Between you and me."

She swallowed.

"Do you feel it too?" he asked, his voice low.

Yes, she mouthed, but no sound came out.

He didn't smile, as she'd expected him to. Instead, his dark brows drew together in a frown. "There's something you should know about me, Skye."

"What's that?" she whispered.

"I . . . I haven't always lived the way I should. I partied hard for a lot of years. Wasn't very respectful of the girls I dated. Never thought it mattered because I didn't have any intention of settling down." He ran a hand over his hair. "God got my attention a few years back, and I've been trying to live right since. It's one of the reasons I came to Kings Meadow. To move away from the man I used to be. I didn't come here to … to get into a serious relationship. I never had plans to fall in love with anybody."

Serious relationship? A warm thrill passed through her. *Fall in love?*

He reached across the corner of the table and took hold of her hand. "I don't know for sure where this is going. Maybe it won't go anywhere. But I'd sure like to find out. Wouldn't you?"

She nodded.

He leaned in slowly, his gaze on her mouth. Unable to breathe, she waited for their lips to meet. The sensations, when it happened, were delicious. She wanted it to last forever. It ended in seconds. But brief as it had been, she knew she would never be the same.

8

Skye was still asleep the next morning when the phone rang.

"Hello?"

"You were supposed to call me when you got back yesterday."

"Hi, Mom." She pushed hair off her face. "I . . . forgot." It was the truth. Her mind had been in a muddle after Grant brought her home late in the afternoon.

"So . . . tell me about your young man."

"It's a little early to start calling him that."

"Is it?"

She remembered the brief kiss in the restaurant. She also remembered the second, slower kiss they'd shared, standing on her doorstep.

"Skye?"

With her free arm, she drew a pillow to her chest and held it close. "Oh, Mom. He's really special. I know nobody's perfect, but I think Grant's perfect for me."

"Tell me about him."

Eyes closed, she launched into a litany of all she'd learned about Grant since the moment they first met. Every wonderful, thrilling, fascinating, charming thing she knew about him.

"My goodness," her mom said when Skye fell silent at last. "He does sound perfect. Doesn't he have *any* flaws?"

Trying to sound more serious and less starstruck, she answered, "He isn't a very good dancer."

"Hmm."

"But we're working on that." Eyes open again, she laughed. She couldn't help it. She was too happy to hold it in for long.

"Your dad and I would love to get to know him. More than to just say hello in church. Could we have you two over for dinner sometime soon?"

"Sure. That'd be great." Skye shoved aside the pillow and sat up. "Sundays and Mondays are his days off. He's pretty busy the rest of the time. Working two jobs and all."

"Well, how about next Sunday after church?"

"Okay. I'll ask him if he's free and let you know." She glanced at the clock and quickly counted the hours until she would meet Grant at the dance studio. Anticipation caused her insides to spin.

Her mom deftly changed the subject, and they chatted for a few more minutes before saying good-bye.

After dropping the phone back into its cradle, Skye was tempted to fall back into bed and pull the sheet over her head. Going back to sleep sounded like the best idea, but something told her it wouldn't happen, even if she tried. Not with Grant's image planted firmly in her mind. She would blame her mom's call, except she'd been dreaming about him when the phone rang.

Smiling, she got out of bed and headed for the shower. Fifteen minutes later, wet hair wrapped in a turban, she stood in front of the bathroom mirror, dressed in her underclothes, and applied makeup. Normally, she was in too much of a hurry to care. A little eye shadow. A bit of mascara. A quick brush of mineral foundation. Even when competing, she'd never been one to primp too much. But today she didn't want to look normal or even settle for pretty. She wanted to look beautiful. For Grant.

Is it real? Can this be happening?

She lowered her hand, still staring at her reflection.

God, I think Grant's the one. I hope he is. Did You bring us together so we can build a future together?

A husband. A home. Babies. Meeting Grant, loving Grant, could mean all of that.

Blessed is the man whose quiver is full of the children of his youth. Isn't that what You say, Lord?

There was that luscious swirl of sensations in her midsection again.

"Mmmm."

She dropped the makeup brush into a bin in the middle drawer, then reached for the blow dryer. If she didn't hurry up, she wouldn't be ready for that lesson with Grant this afternoon.

***

GRANT STOOD BY THE RIVER, SKIPPING SMOOTH, FLAT STONES across the surface of the water. He'd come here to think, not long after the sun was up. It was a quiet setting. Far from any homes or ranches. Far from the road that wound its way east. Most fishermen didn't come to this spot, although Grant didn't know why. He'd seen fish swimming near the banks. But he wasn't about to ask any fishermen. He liked knowing he could come here and be alone, to think and to pray.

This morning, his thoughts and prayers were all about Skye Foster.

It wasn't often that he felt as unsure of himself as he did right now. BC Grant had been arrogant and impudent. The new version of Grant was more levelheaded, more of a clear thinker, more prudent.

Prudent? He skipped another stone. *Not exactly what I'd call what I said and did yesterday.*

Maybe not, but he'd meant it. All of it. He wanted to find out where things might go between them. And he'd meant that kiss too. Those kisses. He was more than attracted to Skye. It wasn't merely the desire of a guy for a beautiful gal. There was more to his feelings than that.

"But can I trust my feelings? The heart's deceitful. Right?"

He tipped his head back and looked beyond his hat brim at the cloudless blue sky, as if expecting to find the answer written in the heavens. It wasn't.

Skye was special. He didn't want to hurt her, but he was afraid he would. This was new territory for him. He'd never expected to meet a girl who could change his mind about love and marriage. Not that Skye *had* changed his mind. Especially not about the latter. Not yet anyway.

But what if she *did* change it and then he discovered—too late—that he wasn't cut out to be one half of a whole?

What if he was meant to be a whole all on his own? Hadn't the apostle Paul written that it was better to be single? Grant didn't have to be like the rest of his family, rushing into love, rushing into marriage, rushing into having kids.

He shook his head as he scuffed his boot against the hard ground. He'd been sure of himself yesterday morning. Why all the doubts now?

Maybe because there's already more between us than I know what to do with. Maybe because it scares me, not knowing what's going to happen next.

He released a deep breath. Scared or not, confused or not, he would be with Skye this afternoon. He would hold her in his arms while the music played and while he tried not to step on her toes.

And if opportunity allowed, he would kiss her again.

Skye came around the corner of her dance studio at a quarter before the hour. The Jeep was parked at the curb. Grant leaned his backside against it, his legs braced, ankles crossed, face shaded by his hat brim.

Add a guitar and it'd make a great album cover.

"You're early again," she said with a smile.

He straightened away from the vehicle. "Guess I'm eager to get the footwork right."

Heart tripping, she put the key in the lock and turned the deadbolt.

"Tell me something," he said from nearby.

"What's that?" The words were nearly inaudible, even to herself.

"You park in the back lot, but you don't go in through the backdoor. How come?"

Well, that wasn't what she'd expected him to ask. It left her disappointed, to say the least. She faced him. "Habit, more than anything. And the lock on the backdoor sticks sometimes, so coming around to the front is easier than fighting with it."

"Mmm." He pulled on the bar to open the door. "Maybe I should look at the lock and get it to stop sticking."

"Sure. If you want to."

Skye led the way inside, Grant following right behind. The interior of the studio was bathed in shadows. It was tempting to leave it that way. More romantic. But she forced herself to open the blinds and let in the sunlight. Best if she remembered why they were here. She'd promised Charity the entire wedding party would be the best dancing bunch this valley had ever seen.

"We're going to work on the two-step today," she said, heading for the stereo. "This is the Two-Step Dance Studio, after all."

"What about that waltz we did last week? I didn't master that yet."

She smiled at the uncertainty in his voice. "You will. We still have time. I want you able to do at least two dances at the wedding. So we'll get the basics of the two-step down this week, and next week we'll start perfecting it and the waltz."

He shook his head slowly but said nothing.

Skye selected a Josh Turner album from her collection of music on the iPod. Punching the control, she fast-forwarded to the last track, "Why Don't We Just Dance." Josh's deep voice came through the speakers.

"Great song," Grant said.

She turned toward him again. "Just listen to it. Get a feel for the tempo. Count it out. One. Two. Three. Four. Five. Six." She patted herself near her collarbone for several bars. "Feel that beat. One. Two. Three. Four. Five. Six. Feel it on your insides."

"Okay. I'm feelin' it."

"We're going to dance to those six beats." She paused the player, plunging the studio into silence. She returned to stand before Grant. "For the man, the first step always starts with his left foot. So put your weight on your right. We're not going to move at first. Just step in place. There are two quick steps, followed by two slow steps."

"How quick?" Unmistakable dread filled his voice.

She couldn't help herself. She took hold of his hands, then rose on tiptoe to kiss him lightly, almost playfully, on the lips. "You can do this. Relax. Okay? Relax."

"Easy for you to say," he muttered—but he was smiling again.

She squeezed his hands before releasing them. "Left is one. Right is two. Left is three, four. Right is five, six. Quick. Quick. Slow. Slow. Ready?"

"As I'll ever be." He took a half step forward. "But when do we get to the part where I get to hold you?"

She laughed. "When you earn it."

"Knew there had to be a catch."

Her mom had always said that falling in love was exhausting because of all the highs and lows involved, but that being in love for the long haul was like a good fire on a cold winter night, full of comfort. Skye wasn't sure about the second part, but the first part was wrong. She found falling in love exhilarating. It was all highs so far.

"Teacher?"

"Hmm."

"I don't think I can wait."

And he didn't. He grabbed the brim of his hat, pulled it off his head, and tossed it aside. Then he placed his index finger under her chin, tipped her head back, and lowered his mouth to hers. Skye felt the kiss all the way down to her toes, and she was grateful when he wrapped his arms around her, lest she crumple into a helpless heap at his feet.

I love you, Grant. I know it's happening fast, but I love you.

He ended the kiss and drew back, though not far. His breath still warmed her cheek. She opened her eyes to look up into his.

"Miss Foster," he said, voice low, "I've completely forgotten the steps."

"Strange, Mr. Nichols. So have I."

9

On matters of a romantic nature, Grant would have preferred to talk to Buck Malone. A year ago, Grant's good friend had been a lot like him when it came to thoughts of marriage. Although for different reasons than Grant, Buck hadn't been interested in settling down with one woman. Meeting Charity had changed his mind.

But Buck was in the backcountry for the next week with a large group of riders, and Grant couldn't wait until his return. He needed advice now. When he arrived at the Leonard Ranch on Thursday, he went looking for Chet. Grant found his boss in a stall in the barn, doctoring a wound on a yearling's chest.

"Mornin'," Grant said as he leaned his arms on the top rail.

Chet glanced up, then returned to his task. "Morning."

"What happened to this young fella?"

"Not sure. Looks like he tangled with barbed wire. But I

had the boys look for loose wire or a downed fence, and they couldn't find anything."

Grant placed a boot on the bottom rail. "Any changes in our plans for the rest of the week?"

"Nope. You'll be doing all of your cooking at the chef's patio. No trail rides. Lunch and dinner today. Dinners only the rest of the week." Chet straightened and patted the yearling's neck. "Do you need help? Sam's around if you want him to join you."

"No thanks. I'm good." He took a few steps back as Chet reached for the gate. "But I was wondering if you had a minute to talk."

"Sure. What's up?" Chet came out of the stall.

"I . . . I . . ." Grant took a slow, deep breath. "It's about Skye Foster."

Chet cocked an eyebrow. "What about her?"

"Well, I—" Why did he feel so tongue tied? *Spit it out, already.* "To tell you the truth, Chet, I think I'm falling in love with her."

"Yeah?"

"No. Not quite right. I think I've *fallen* in love with her. Past tense. Already happened."

"And the problem is . . . ?" Chet leaned a shoulder against the stall.

Grant removed his hat and ran a hand over his hair. "I don't know that there is one. But it all happened so fast. I've never known anyone like her before. And I knew plenty of girls before I came to Idaho. I hooked up with someone different at every party, without any intention of ever seeing any of them again. That's why I haven't dated since I got here. I thought it better to give all women a wide berth while

I turned my life around. I didn't want to fall into my old patterns."

"I know. I thought it a sound plan."

"Chet, I never planned to get married. I figured I'd stay a bachelor the rest of my life."

His friend chuckled. "But you're thinking about marriage anyway."

"Yeah. I guess I am. I mean, that's the only place love can lead for a Christian couple. Right?"

"I'd say that's true. If that's what God has for you and Skye."

Grant walked to the far end of the barn and looked out at the paddocks beyond the open doors. *"If that's what God has for you and Skye."* If marriage was what God wanted for them, then everything would work out. The things he worried about now wouldn't matter anymore.

Chet arrived at his side.

"When I'm with her," Grant said softly, "I don't have any doubts. Except about my dancing." They both chuckled. "When I'm with her, all I want is to stay with her. To be with her all the time. To hear her laughter. To listen to her talk . . . about *anything*. She's interesting and funny, and we like the same music and books. We both like the outdoors. She'll always want to own horses and so will I. Having them will probably keep us strapped for cash but neither of us will care. We don't have expensive tastes. It's like—" He shrugged. "It's like we were meant for each other."

"Maybe you are."

Grant finally cracked a smile. "But you're not going to tell me what to do, are you?"

"No." Chet shook his head. "You'll have to wrestle

through your questions with God. I'm not in the match-making business." He chuckled again. "But I will tell you this: when I fell in love with Kimberly, I didn't think it was going to work out between us. Unlike you and Skye, we had lots of differences that seemed certain to keep us apart. But God has a way of cutting through the stuff we think is impossible. He'll do the same for you, if you're listening to Him."

"And you don't think this has happened too fast between us?"

"It all depends, I suppose. But I've known more than one couple who fell in love in a matter of days or weeks and who are still married after thirty or forty or even fifty years. I know another couple that courted for years, and they were divorced before the first year was out. I'm not saying you should rush. I'm saying there's no set timetable. God's timing is what matters. Not yours."

Strange, the calmness that fell over him. As if all of his questions had been answered. As if all of his worries had been swept away.

"Thanks, Chet. You've been a big help."

***

Skye rode River out of the arena and walked him toward the lean-to. Once there, she dismounted and quickly set about removing saddle and bridle.

"You're going to be a champ," she said as she slipped the halter on him. "Aren't you, boy?"

The horse's ears flicked forward and he turned his head away from her. She had to follow right along with him in order to fasten the buckle. That's when she saw Grant walking toward her.

An already perfect day got instantly better.

"Hey, Skye." Small clouds of dirt rose behind his boots as he walked.

"Hey, Grant." Her heart did a little trill in her chest.

They had spoken on the phone several times since his last dance lesson, but this was the first she'd seen him in person in several days. It surprised her, how the sight of him made her feel.

"River looked great out there," he said, stopping nearby.

"You saw?"

"Some. I stayed in my Jeep. Didn't want to take a chance of disturbing him." He paused. "Or you."

One more thing to love about Grant. He knew better than to interrupt a horse in training. He was willing and able to be patient.

She said, "I thought you were working all day at the Leonards'."

"I am. But I wanted to see you before I start cooking again."

She didn't know if she should be delighted or worried. Was it something urgent? Or was it something he'd rather not say over the phone? Such as he couldn't go to her parents' home for Sunday dinner. Her mom would be disappointed if that was what he'd come to say.

"Come here, you." He took hold of her upper arms and drew her to him. "There. That's better." He embraced her, holding her close.

"I'm all horsey."

"I like horsey." He kissed her on the forehead.

"And gritty."

"I'll take my chances." He lowered his head so their lips could meet. A long, slow, luscious kiss.

River snorted hard, spraying them both.

They broke apart. Neither of them spoke. Then, in unison, they laughed.

"River," Grant said, "you're a real killjoy." He reached for Skye's left hand and drew her away from the lean-to and the horse. "I've got something important to say, and I need your full attention."

She sobered. "Okay. You've got it." Her mouth went dry, and she found it hard to swallow.

"Skye Foster, since the day I met you, I haven't been able to think straight."

Now she didn't seem able to breathe.

"But I feel like I know you better than some people I've known my whole life. I told you last Sunday that I wanted to see where things might go between us. That's not quite true anymore."

"It isn't?" she whispered.

"No, because I already know where it's going. I already know what I feel." He took a half step closer to her. "Call me crazy if you want, but . . . I love you."

He loves me?

"I've never said that to a woman before. Never said it to anybody who isn't a member of my family. Never."

You haven't?

"I'd like you to become a member of my family, Skye. Will you marry me?"

Vision blurred by unexpected tears, Skye's happiness bubbled over into laughter. Grant took a step back from her, and she realized he thought she was laughing at him, at his proposal.

"Wait. Grant. No. I mean, yes. Yes, I'll marry you."

"You will? Wahoo!"

He picked her up underneath the arms and spun her around and around. Her legs flew out like swings at the carnival. The first thing he did when he set her down was to kiss her again. Only the kiss was different this time. The kiss claimed her for his own. She felt winded by the time he straightened.

"I've gotta get back to work," he said. "I don't want to, but I've got to."

"I know. It's all right. Go."

"I don't have a ring for you yet."

"It's okay."

"Can I come to your house tonight when I'm done at the Tamarack? It'll be late."

She grinned. "That's okay too. I'll wait up."

IT WAS CLOSE TO MIDNIGHT BEFORE GRANT PULLED HIS JEEP into Skye's driveway. The light above the front stoop was on, shedding a warm yellow glow several feet in all directions. Another light inside the house told him he was expected.

He hopped out of the vehicle and strode to the front door. Rather than ring the bell, he rapped lightly. The door opened in seconds. Skye looked up at him, eyes sleepy. Or would he call them dreamy?

"Hey, beautiful."

"Hi." She shoved tousled hair back from her face.

"You were asleep."

"On the sofa."

He cupped the side of her face, leaned forward, and kissed her. "I shouldn't have asked you to wait up."

"Yes, you should have. I needed to see you. I needed to know I wasn't dreaming earlier today."

"You weren't dreaming."

Holding onto the front of his shirt, she drew him over the threshold. He caught the open door with his fingertips and swiped it closed. He became instantly aware of how alone they were in this little bungalow. He remembered how easy it could be—with the right words, with the right look in his eyes, with the pressure of his lips—to help a girl let down her defenses.

Careful, he warned himself. *Be careful.*

"Would you like something to drink?" she asked, intruding on the silence. "There's Coke in the fridge, or I could make some decaf."

He wasn't thirsty, but a little distance between them might be a good thing. "Decaf would be great."

"I'll get it for you."

She turned and headed into the kitchen. He followed a few moments behind. On the opposite side of the kitchen bar, he sat on a stool and watched as she filled the carafe with water and poured it into the coffeemaker's reservoir.

"Did you tell anybody?" he asked at last.

She faced him but stayed where she was. "No. I didn't know if you wanted me to yet." She tipped her head slightly to one side. "Did you tell anyone?"

"No." He smiled. "But it was hard not to with so many people in and out of the kitchen tonight. I thought I'd explode with the news. I didn't expect that. Then again, I didn't expect any of this. People tried to tell me it would be like this. My parents. My brothers and sisters. Have I mentioned the Nicholses are a romantic lot? I didn't think I got that particular gene, but I was wrong."

"Not sure you told me about them being romantics. However, I can tell your parents raised you with good manners. When I'm with you I feel . . . protected." She returned his smile. "Cherished."

Who knew it would feel this good to hear her say something like that? And it made him determined to keep her feeling protected and cherished, determined not to hurt her or abuse her trust in even the smallest of ways.

"Grant?"

"Hmm." It was hard not to get off the stool and go take her in his arms again.

"Let's wait to tell anybody here in Kings Meadow until after we have dinner with my parents on Sunday. Is that all right with you? I'd like the two of us to tell them in person first."

The sounds and scent of coffee brewing filled the kitchen.

"Sure. That's fine with me. Do you think they'll take it all right? It happening so fast, I mean."

She nodded. "I think so. As soon as they really get to meet you, they'll know we're right for each other."

"I'll wait to call my parents until Sunday night."

"Will they take it all right?"

He chuckled. "All they'll want to know is when do they get to meet you and how soon is the wedding." Surprise shot through him when he realized how he wanted to answer them. "Can I tell them it will be soon?"

Her large, dark eyes widened, all traces of sleepiness long gone. "How soon?"

"How about at the end of September or early October?"

She walked toward him, stopping with the bar still between them. "Yes. The colors will be turning by then. A perfect backdrop for a wedding. It will be beautiful."

"*You're* beautiful." He leaned across the kitchen bar and kissed her. "It may sound corny, Skye, but you've made me the happiest guy on earth."

10

The way Skye felt, she couldn't believe the entire congregation couldn't see the truth for themselves. It was a wonder everyone didn't come over at the end of the service and start shaking Grant's hand and congratulating them both.

But if anyone guessed she and Grant were engaged, no one let on, and the couple made it to her parents' home with their secret still intact. The next half an hour was pure agony while her mom and dad asked Grant questions and he answered them. But Skye could only hold back the announcement for so long.

When a lull in the conversation occurred, she reached over and took hold of Grant's hand. "Mom. Dad. Grant and I have something to tell you." She tightened her grip. "We're getting married."

"What?" her dad exclaimed.

Her mom shushed him. "Let her talk, Rand."

"We know it seems fast," Skye said. "We've only known

each other a few weeks. But we're sure, Dad. We love each other. And we aren't rushing straight to the altar. We thought this fall would be a good time for the wedding."

Grant cleared his throat. "Sir, I love your daughter." He looked at her father with a steady gaze. "I'm as sure of that as I've ever been sure of anything. I promise I'll take care of her, be a good husband to her, cherish her always. You've got my word on it." He put an arm around her shoulders and tugged her close.

Her dad was quiet for a long while, then said, "Neither one of you are kids. You're old enough to make decisions for yourselves. I don't know you well, Grant, but I respect the men who are your friends. That says a lot about you too. And Skye, you know your own mind. I never had to worry about you the way I worried about your brother and sister. You were always more focused and self-disciplined than they were. So if this is what you want, then God bless you. I hope you'll both be as happy as your mom and I have been all these years."

Tears slipped down Skye's cheeks as she got up to hug her father. When she turned toward her mom, she saw that she was sniffling. Happy tears, judging by the smile on her lips.

After they'd exchanged a hug, too, her mom said, "I'd best get that roast out of the oven before it turns to charcoal."

"I'll help." Skye took two steps toward the kitchen, stopped, and turned to look once again at Grant. After several heartbeats, she mouthed the words, *I love you.* Then she left the room, her heart tripping with joy.

THE MEAL WAS OVER, BUT THEY LINGERED AT THE DINING ROOM table over cups of coffee. Grant felt accepted by Skye's parents. No small thing. It was easy to envision a future full of friendly dinners like this one.

Midge rose from her chair and began to clear the table. Skye got up to help her. Soon, running water and the clatter of plates and clink of glasses could be heard from the kitchen.

"I'll get the rest of these dishes," Grant said to Rand.

When he arrived at the doorway, he paused to look at the two women, mother and daughter, as they worked. It reminded him of home and his mom and sisters.

"I can hardly wait to meet Grant's family," Skye was saying. "Especially his mother. She raised ten kids, Mom. Ten. She must be full of advice, and I plan to ask her all kinds of questions when we get to meet. You know how I've always dreamed of having a big family like the one Grant grew up in. Oh, Mom. I can hardly wait until we have babies of our own. We'll have a big old house with a rope swing in the tree in the backyard and ponies for the kids to ride when they're little."

Grant went cold all over. He knew Skye and her mother continued to talk, but their voices were more like a buzz in his ears now.

He and Skye had crammed a lot of information, questions, and answers into the short time they'd known each other. Whenever together, they'd talked. About everything. How was it possible she'd never said anything about wanting a big family like his? Never a clue that she was eager to add to the overpopulation of the world. But then, he couldn't lay the blame at her feet. He should have made his own sentiments clear when he proposed. Or better yet, before he proposed. Why hadn't he thought to tell her how he felt about it?

A sick knot formed in his gut.

Midge Foster caught sight of him in the doorway. "Oh, thank you, Grant. That was nice of you to bring those to us."

Feeling stiff, he moved forward and set the dishes on the counter next to the sink.

As he turned, Skye touched the back of one of his hands with her fingertips. "I'll help Mom clean up, and then we can go."

He nodded.

To her mom, Skye said, "We're going to call Grant's parents with the news after we leave here."

"Grant, I look forward to meeting your parents. I hope your whole family can come down for the wedding."

The whole family. Thirty-two of them, counting spouses. Where would they all stay if they did come? Kings Meadow didn't have a motel. Only a bed-and-breakfast that had three available bedrooms. He knew because that's where he'd stayed upon his arrival in town.

His head began to throb.

Maybe he hadn't prayed about this marriage idea enough. Maybe he hadn't heard God's answer after all. He'd given Rand Foster his word that he would take care of Skye, that he would make her happy. They weren't even wed yet— not even home yet—and he was about to break that promise.

⸻

Tension emanated from Grant. Almost like a third entity in the Jeep.

When Skye dared to glance at him, his eyes were locked on the street ahead, his mouth set in a hard line. His hands gripped the steering wheel as if he might try to break it in two.

Something had gone awry, and she didn't know what. There had been joy and laughter at her parents' home throughout the dinner. Announcing their engagement plans had gone even better than she'd hoped it would. But something had changed before they left the house.

She didn't have the courage to ask Grant about it. She would have to wait until he told her of his own accord.

However long that'll be.

As soon as the Jeep stopped in her driveway, Skye opened the passenger door before Grant, per usual, could come around and open it for her. His tension had become her tension, and she couldn't stand to wait for him. Wordlessly, she led the way up the narrow walk.

"I'll be out in a minute," she said over her shoulder as she headed to her bedroom. Once inside, she closed the door and leaned against it, her breath rapid and shallow. *Calm down. You don't know anything's wrong. Not for sure.*

He loved her. That was what mattered. That was all that mattered. Wasn't it?

She pushed off the door, stepped over to the mirror above her dresser, and stared at her reflection. Forcing herself to take a slow, deep breath, then another, she pushed her hair behind her shoulders.

Yes, that was better. Foolish to stand in here, imagining the worst. Better to go out and talk to Grant. That was what people did when they were married. They talked things through. Might as well begin now.

Drawing one more deep breath, she left the bedroom and walked the short hallway to the living room. Grant stood at the window, staring outside, his thumbs tucked into the back pockets of his jeans.

"Are we ready to make that phone call?" she asked, trying to sound normal, not sure she succeeded.

He turned toward her. "We need to talk first."

Dread became a lump in her chest. "Okay." She expected him to move to the sofa where they could sit, side by side, as they discussed whatever was on his mind. He didn't. He stayed near the window, the light at his back, casting his face in shadows.

"I heard . . . I heard you talking to your mom. In the kitchen before we left. I heard you say you want a big family. I saw how much joy that idea gave you. You came alive when you talked about it. It was written all over your face."

She nodded, glad that he understood her so well, still afraid because she didn't know what he would say next.

"Skye, we never talked about kids. I don't think I can give you what you want."

This time she shook her head, confused.

"I never planned on having kids of my own," he said softly. "No big family for me. I can't."

"Can't?" Was there a medical reason? Because if—

"Won't." The single word dashed her brief hope. "I decided a long time ago. No kids."

Tears welled, and she rubbed them away. "You decided," she whispered, the words like a dagger to her chest.

"Maybe I'd better go so you can think about it. So we

both can think about it. I'm sorry, Skye. Real sorry. It's just . . . I don't know . . . I just—" He broke off, frustration obvious, and walked to the door. Without looking back at her, he said, "I'll call you."

The instant the door closed, she sank to the floor. Tears flowed down her cheeks, but she didn't sob. Didn't make a sound. She hadn't the strength for more than one single thought.

So this is what a broken heart feels like.

11

Grant arranged for time off from both of his jobs and was on the road to Montana before dawn the next morning. It was a little better than a six-hour drive, taking the route through the mountains and not counting any stops for fuel or food. He pulled into the barnyard of the Nichols family ranch just after one o'clock in the afternoon.

Before he could close the door to his Jeep, his mom was running toward him from the house. "Grant! Grant's here!" she shouted to anyone within hearing distance. In the next instant, she was hugging him. "Oh, son, you're home again. You're home. It's been too long."

"Hey, Mom."

"Why didn't you let us know you were coming?" she asked as she drew back from him.

"It was a last-minute decision. Spur of the moment."

His dad appeared out of the barn. A second or two later, Vince came around the corner of the house. More hugs were exchanged. More questions about his impromptu visit. His answers were evasive, although honest.

He might have fooled his parents as per the nature of his visit, but not his older brother. "Care to tell me what's up?" Vince asked as soon as they were alone in the room they'd shared as boys.

Grant dropped his duffle on the bed. He'd had all those hours of driving to think about what had happened with Skye. Not only what had happened yesterday but from the first moment he'd met her. Thinking hadn't solved the dilemma. Maybe talking about it would. Maybe.

He sat on the bed. "I met a girl," he began.

After that the words poured out of him. Vince listened, never trying to interrupt. Not even once. He didn't make a sound until Grant ran out of words. All he said then was, "Wow."

"Wow? I was hoping for something more than that."

"Wow. I had no idea you were such a bonehead. How's that for something more?"

Grant wasn't sure how to respond.

"Look, bro. I know being part of a big family isn't always easy. And being the oldest two kids meant a lot of stuff fell on our shoulders, yours and mine, when we were growing up. But you're no prize, you know. Yeah, you've turned your life around in the last few years. I'm proud of you for it. But you've got more work to do in that head of yours. You think Mom and Dad had too many kids? You think your brothers and sisters all married too young and had their own kids too fast? Who made you the judge?"

Wasn't Vince ever going to draw a breath?

"Maybe you oughta take another look at this family,

Grant. Yeah, we're big and noisy. Yeah, at any family gathering there's probably at least one baby crying and another needing a diaper change. But there are also husbands and wives there, supporting each other, loving each other, helping each other. Because of the examples of our parents, we've got strong marriages that we keep working on so that they'll stay strong. And there isn't a single one of your brothers and sisters who wouldn't do just about anything for you if you needed them. If you were in trouble, there'd be an entire tribe coming to your rescue. How many people in this world are lucky enough to say the same?"

Defensive, Grant said, "I never said I didn't love and appreciate my family."

"Then start taking note of your blessings. And then check with your brain and your heart to see if you even know what you want anymore. Don't stay a bonehead. Grow up!" With those words, Vince strode out of the room.

"What got him so riled?" Grant muttered.

He tried to get angry over his brother's outburst, but he failed. In fact, something in his gut told him they were the words he'd driven all the way from Kings Meadow to hear.

———

Skye pressed her face again Snickers' neck. She would have wept, but her tears had run dry after four days of doing little else but crying.

Grant's last words to her had been that he would call.

He hadn't called.

He hadn't come to his dance lesson on Monday night.

And yesterday she'd learned from Chet Leonard that Grant had gone to Montana. For a few days? Or for good?

"Skye."

She gasped softly. Now she was hearing voices. No, now she was hearing *his* voice.

"Skye?"

She spun around, and there he stood—black hat, rumpled cotton shirt tucked into the waistband of his jeans, boots covered in a fine layer of dust.

He took a step forward. "Can we talk?"

"If you want." She turned toward the gelding and stroked his neck.

"My brother called me a bonehead. He was right. I am one."

After all the crying she'd done in the past few days, the urge to laugh took her completely by surprise. It even maddened her. She looked over her shoulder and followed him with her eyes as he walked to the opposite side of Snickers.

"I was wrong not to sit down and talk it through, you and me, right then, Sunday night. I panicked, I guess. I love you, but all of a sudden I saw my whole world spiraling out of control."

"I'm sorry," she said stiffly. "I didn't mean to do that to you."

"No. You misunderstood. That's not what I meant." He ran a hand over his face. "Man, I'm making a mess of it."

Skye couldn't argue with that.

He leaned against Snickers's side. "But maybe it was for the best, me going away for a few days. Maybe I needed my one and only big brother to knock some sense into me. Maybe he's the only one who could."

"Did he?" Hope rose in her chest.

"Yes."

"Like what?"

"Like looking at all the ways God's blessed me through that big, noisy, interfering, exasperating family of mine. Like holding one of my nieces in my arms and realizing the absolute miracle of new life. Like how much I love you. Really love you. Deep down in my bones love you." His arm snaked across the horse's back, and he clasped Skye's right hand in his left. "Skye, I don't know if I'd ever be ready to have as many kids as my folks did. But when the time's right, I wouldn't mind starting with one . . . as long as you're the mother."

"Oh, Grant," she whispered.

"Stay there."

He hurried around Snickers and stopped before her. She thought he was about to hug her, but instead, he drew her into a dance hold, his right hand in the small of her back, warm, strong, reassuring.

He stared down at her. "I want to dance with you for the rest of my life, Skye." He started to sway side to side. "But you know I've got two left feet. I'm going to need you to teach me the steps, and you know I'm gonna stumble every now and again. Probably step on your toes. Think you can handle it?"

Soft laughter escaped her. "Grant, remember what I told you the first time we met? I love a challenge." She pressed her cheek against his chest. "As long as we dance together, we're going to be just fine."

EPILOGUE

Through tear-blurred eyes, Skye watched the wedding party—bride and groom, parents of the bride and groom, best man and maid of honor, groomsmen and bridesmaids—waltz around the dance floor. Who wouldn't cry at such a beautiful moment?

Everything about this wedding had been sublime. Just as she'd imagined it would be—the bride and groom speaking their vows in the gazebo, the morning sun bathing the world in a golden July glow, the guests filling row after row of white folding chairs, the cutting of the cake, the music, and now the dancing.

The waltz ended. Skye looked for Grant. He'd been with the wedding party a moment before, dancing with one of the bridesmaids. But now she couldn't see him. Where had he gone? Then, seemingly out of nowhere, he stood before her. Still wearing his suit jacket but with the addition of a gray cowboy hat covering his hair.

"Care to risk your feet, Miss Foster?" A slow grin curved his mouth.

"I'm a brave woman, Mr. Nichols."

"Yes, you are."

She stepped into his arms as the band began to play "I Hope You Dance."

Perfect.

She loved the way Grant made her feel as he folded her smaller hand within his larger one. There was a sense of security in his other hand against the small of her back. Her heart fluttered as they moved in time to the music.

Heavenly.

She tilted her head back and looked up at him. Beneath the brim of his gray Stetson, she saw the love in his eyes and the warmth of his smile. No shadows could hide him from her. She saw him as clearly as he saw her, and the knowledge made her tremble with more happiness than she had ever dreamed possible.

Skye had learned something important over the summer. Dreams for her future were all well and good, but the present—whatever that present looked like—was what she was meant to embrace, to savor.

Here, in the arms of the man she loved was the only dance, the only moment, that mattered.

Foster Family Tree

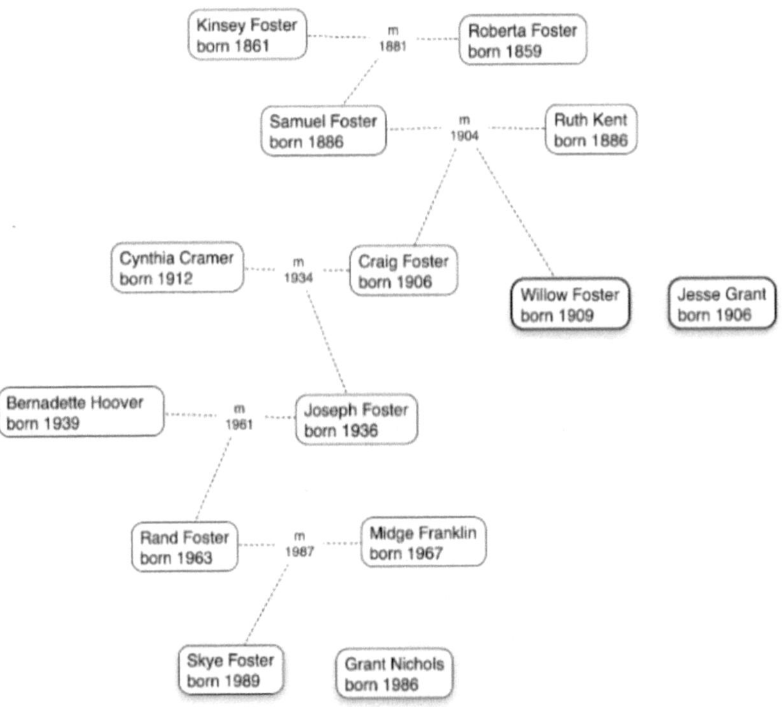

ABOUT THE AUTHOR

Robin Lee Hatcher is the best-selling author of over 95 books. Her well-drawn characters and heartwarming stories of faith, courage, and love have earned her both critical acclaim and the devotion of readers. Her numerous awards include the Christy Award, the RITA® Award, Romantic Times Career Achievement Awards for Americana Romance and for Inspirational Fiction, the Carol Award, and Lifetime Achievement Awards from both Romance Writers of America® (2001) and American Christian Fiction Writers (2014).

When not writing, Robin enjoys being with her family, spending time in the beautiful Idaho outdoors, Bible art journaling, reading books that make her cry, watching romantic movies, knitting, and decorative planning. A mother and grandmother, Robin makes her home on the outskirts of Boise, sharing it with a demanding Papillon dog.

Learn more about Robin and her books and subscribe to her newsletter on her website at robinleehatcher.com

ALSO BY ROBIN LEE HATCHER

Stand Alone Titles

Like the Wind

I'll Be Seeing You

Words Matter

Make You Feel My Love

An Idaho Christmas

Here in Hart's Crossing

The Victory Club

Beyond the Shadows

Catching Katie

Whispers From Yesterday

The Shepherd's Voice

Ribbon of Years

Firstborn

The Forgiving Hour

Heart Rings

A Wish and a Prayer

When Love Blooms

A Carol for Christmas

Return to Me

Loving Libby

Wagered Heart

The Perfect Life

Speak to Me of Love

Trouble in Paradise

Another Chance to Love You

Bundle of Joy

The British Are Coming

To Enchant a Lady's Heart

To Marry an English Lord

To Capture a Mountain Man

Boulder Creek Romance

Even Forever

All She Ever Dreamed

The Coming to America Series

Dear Lady

Patterns of Love

In His Arms

Promised to Me

Where the Heart Lives Series

Belonging

Betrayal

Beloved

Books set in Kings Meadow

A Promise Kept

Love Without End

Whenever You Come Around

I Hope You Dance

Keeper of the Stars

Bible and a .44/From This Moment On

Books set in Thunder Creek

You'll Think of Me

You're Gonna Love Me

The Sisters of Bethlehem Springs Series

A Vote of Confidence

Fit to Be Tied

A Matter of Character

Legacy of Faith series

Who I am With You

Cross My Heart

How Sweet It Is

For a full list of books, visit robinleehatcher.com